Advance praise for *Everything Is Totally Fine*

"The stories on pages 3, 14, 22, 24, 29, 31, 34, 41, 43, 56, 62, 64, 76, 87, 89, 93, 96, 97, 103, 105, 107, 110, 111, 115, 118, 121, 122, 124, 126, 135, 143, 144, 146 made me laugh. The stories on pages 3, 12, 22, 27, 29, 31, 34, 39, 43, 49, 54, 56, 58, 62, 69, 72, 74, 75, 76, 83, 86, 87, 93, 97, 103, 114, 122, 126, 135, 140 caused me to feel pleasantly heartached in their relation of truths I've either observed independently, or that I came to understand about life, as I read. The stories on pages 3, 14, 29, 34, 41, 43, 49, 56, 62, 64, 75, 76, 83, 89, 93, 96, 103, 107, 110, 111, 115, 118, 124, 126, 135, 144 struck me as original, imaginative, and surprising (tonally, structurally, and/or in subject matter); I had no idea where these stories were going. The main image of the story on page 43 has popped into my mind around ten times since reading this collection two months ago; I think about it often when driving. After reading the stories on pages 29, 93, 144, I handed the book to another person who I excitedly told to 'read this,' who did so and laughed, said things like 'what the fuck,' and read sentences aloud that had also delighted me when I'd read them."

—Megan Boyle, author of *Liveblog*

"Stories that will surprise you again and again with touching revelations about the lonely insanity of our world. Refreshingly bold and insane."

—Mark Leidner, author of *Returning the Sword to the Stone*

"Apocalyptic fire, gnostic world-hatred and the philosophy of futility reveal themselves in mundane absurdities and banalities. Zac Smith shows us that we're still not nihilistic enough; we're still too hopeful. This book sends out dark but mirthful energy waves into the night."

—Lars Iyer, author of *Nietzsche and the Burbs*

"Zac's book helped me see the world in new and surprising ways, which is my favorite thing books can do. These stories are lovely."

—Andrew Weatherhead, author of *$50,000*

EVERYT HING IS TOTAL LY FINE !!!!!!!!!!!!!!

EVERYT HING IS TOTAL LY FINE

Stories by
Zac Smith

Muumuu House
muumuuhouse.com

EVERYTHING IS TOTALLY FINE

Muumuu House
Second edition, February 2022

978-0982206768
0982206763

Cover design by Giacomo Pope

The following stories have appeared, in slightly different forms, in the following places online: "Bugs," "Public Transportation," and "Scaffolding" in *X-R-A-Y Lit*; "Doors," "Hold Music," "Like a Car That Looks Exactly Like a Slightly Smaller Car," "Stretch Your Arms. Stretch Your Fingers. Stretch Your Back. Think About Your Body. Think About Your Body in Freefall. You're Free!," and "The Literary Agent," in *Hobart*; "Tree" (as "Birds") in *Instant Lit*; "Healthy, Fit, and Fulfilled" in *New World Writing*; "The First Millennial President" in *Bending Genres*; "The Very Good Dog" in *Young Mag*; "Tomatoes" and "This Fucking Dresser" in *Forever Mag*; "Loss" in *Philosophical Idiot*; "Normal Life 2," "What a Disaster!," and "Today Is Totally Fucked 1" in *Wigleaf*; and "A Beautiful Hill" and "Putting Yourself Out There Just to Make Room for Yourself Version 2.0" in *Neutral Spaces*.

Everything Is Totally Fucked

Everything Is Totally Fine

Everything Is Normal Life

Everything Is

Totally Fucked

Today Is Totally Fucked 2

Broke the coffee pot (shitty coffee pot). Just the glass part. Not the plastic part. Not the part where the glugging sound comes from, like, where the coffee comes out. The glass part, where the coffee goes, that's the part I broke. But it's an important part. The whole thing is unusable.

Eating five cookies. There's no coffee. And I'm so thirsty. I can barely breathe, because of all the crumbs from the cookies, and there's no coffee or water (the sink is also broken).

My kids are asking where the coffee is. I have to make something up. I lie to them. I tell them the coffee is on its way. They ask about the glugging sound—there's no glugging sound—and I try to glug for them while looking away. I look at the wall, then the place where the coffee pot is. I try to obscure the broken glass and make a glugging sound with my mouth. But the crumbs. Cookie crumbs. It comes out like this: *klukha kha spatka kla.* They press the issue: *that's not a glugging sound.* I'm starting to freak out. I think about the phrase *starting to freak out.* I feel like I'm starting to freak out but in a way where it's spelled *stratting to frake out.* I can't swallow any of the cookies. I try to spit out the crumbs. Too many cookies. Can't breathe. The kids can't breathe either. No, they're okay. *Straking to frrk out.* I've been breathing the whole time. I'm trying to glug, also. *Klkha pla pla tspkla.* The kids keep saying things but I can't understand them. There's crumbs and glass and no fucking coffee.

"There's no fucking coffee!" I yell. But it sounds like this: *keres mo flugling khalkfla.* The kids don't know what the fuck.

I open and close the cabinets (shitty cabinets). I think that's something you should do in this situation, like, from a movie I saw once. An instructional video? I see that there are more cookies. Oh my god, there are, like, eight more cookies in the cabinet. I think about my parents. They died when I was fourteen. I try to cram the eight cookies into my mouth while turning around, slowly. I look at my kids with one wide-open eye while eating thirteen cookies and they look at me and they all look like one big face and the face is mouthing the words: *graalgha plargol nngaa.* And I feel nervous because I don't know what that means.

When You Die, Someone Will Rip Off Your Head and Place it Apathetically Onto an Altar Dedicated to Your Ripped-off Head

I built a rocket ship out of old tires and gasoline. I tried following some guides on the internet but I couldn't really afford all the real stuff. I talked to people on the internet about it and eventually got confirmation that the tires and gasoline would work. I had a lot of tires and I could easily buy a lot of gasoline. The rocket ship seemed fully functional. It was getting positive feedback on Instagram. I wanted to fly to the upper atmosphere and look. I had a lot of tires and nothing else to do. And I wanted to see space. I started the rocket ship and held onto the steering wheel while everything rumbled. It was loud. I was worried about not being able to get back home. But it was fine, everything worked out perfectly. Space looked beautiful. I can't really describe it. It was blue, and black, and other colors, and big. But I landed in California, which is, like, six states away. When I got home, I had to take the recycling out. I was listening to a news podcast about my rocket ship. I carried an armload of cardboard and an empty gallon jug down the driveway but the wind blew the jug out of the crook of my arm before I could put it in the bin. The wind made the jug continue to roll up the driveway at a constant speed. I could hear the sound of the jug rolling on the concrete through my earbuds. I chased it at almost the same speed it was rolling. I wasn't catching up. I felt like I would always be chasing the jug. I laughed at how loud and stupid everything was.

Tomatoes

I stood at the crosswalk with a bag of tomatoes. I pushed the button to activate the crosswalk signal. I waited for a car to run the red light and the very first car to drive up ran the red light so I tossed a tomato into the air above the crosswalk. The tomato hit the car's windshield and exploded. I don't know makes or models of cars. It was white and had four doors. It had tomato juice all over the windshield and hood. The driver slammed on the brakes and turned the wheel so the car's front right tire bumped into the curb. The driver tried to get out of the car but the car was still in drive, so he stopped mid-exit to crouch down and go back into the car to shift it into park, then fully exited the car. He started yelling at me about whether I was crazy or whatever. A cop ran his cruiser onto the curb in front of the guy's car and tried to get out of the cruiser but the cruiser was still in drive, so he stopped mid-exit to crouch down and go back into the cruiser to shift it into park, then fully exited the cruiser. He held up his gun and started yelling about whether the guy was crazy or something. I wanted to try to get out of a car but the car was still in drive, so I stopped mid-exit to crouch down and go back into the car to shift it into park, then fully exited the car...or something, whatever would make that sentence work, I don't know. I'm tired. The cop seemed incredibly drunk and kept slurring his words. The guy tried to explain what had happened while still yelling. The cop yelled back trying to tell the guy to stop yelling. I realized that I was also yelling, just really quietly, almost in a whisper, and mostly to myself. The cop started kind of screeching instead of yelling and he leveled his gun at the guy and clicked off the safety. Cars were slowly backing up all around the intersection in all directions. I thought about the line of cars going all the way from the intersection to the West Coast, two thousand miles away. I thought about throwing a tomato at the cop. I thought about trying to steal the gun from the cop. I thought about shooting the cop four times and then packing the bullet wounds with tomatoes. The cop started arresting the man against the hood of the car. The cop rubbed the man against the tomato guts. The cop put the man in the back of his cruiser. The cop closed the door of the cruiser. The cop drove away while firing his gun out the window. An hour later a tow truck came for the car and I went home. I ate tomatoes. Every time I bit into a tomato, it killed every cop in America. I killed every cop in America something like twenty or twenty-five times.

Your Heartbeat as a Depressed Man Repeatedly Smashing His Face Against the 18th-Floor Glass Window

I drove my car really fast and turned the wheel so that the car hit the rail and flipped elegantly off the side of an overpass. My car flew through the air across from twelve children standing on the side of the road. Several of them pointed and one of them said, "Woah, cool" and they all watched my car land upside down on the other side of the road. The gas tank exploded and parts of the car and parts of my body scattered all over the pavement. A school shooter who attended the same school as the children but who hadn't seen me flip my car off the overpass walked up to them and killed them all with an automatic weapon. He listened to their pained screams and watched their blood and organs spill all over the pavement. When I landed and died instantly, I didn't feel any better than I did before. When the children watched me die and blow apart, they didn't feel any better than they did before. When the school shooter killed all of the children, he didn't feel any better than he did before.

I'm Not Here to Commit Any Crimes

The first family I found was camping in an RV near the woods.

"Woof woof," I said to the little girl playing with a toy monster truck near the campfire.

"Doggie!" she said, and ran over.

Her mother stepped out of the camper with a metal spatula, looked at me, and started yelling. She told me to get the fuck away from her daughter. I stepped back and held up my hands like a person does, which means: Everything's cool, I'm not here to commit any crimes.

"Sorry," I said, "I'm a dog."

"Doggie!" said the girl.

"That's right," I said. I smiled, even though dogs don't smile unless it's hot out, and it wasn't that hot out. I was trying to look nice.

The mom told me I wasn't a dog. But she didn't sound really confident.

The dad came out of the RV holding a big stick with a feather tied to the top of it with some twine. It looked like a fun camping craft activity. He looked nervous. It felt like he didn't know what was happening. But if he were a dog, he would have barked at me and bared his teeth and I would have known to run off scared. Or, if I thought I could take him, I would bare my teeth and wrestle with him on the ground to prove it. I would grab him by the neck and start kicking at his stomach. I would try to break the skin and pull out his intestines. I would try to bite his neck and face until he whimpered off and died. But we both just stood there looking at each other instead, like people do. It's different but, like, also the same thing kind of.

I asked them if they wanted to adopt a dog. I was talking about myself. I wanted them to adopt me. The dog. The mom told me to leave. That meant no.

"Okay," I said. The dad didn't say anything. He looked relieved.

"Bye, Doggie!" the little girl said. She waved goodbye. I turned and walked back into the woods.

This Fucking Dresser

⌒

I posted a dresser for free on Craigslist. Two college kids wearing gym shorts came for it. They took all the drawers out of the dresser and put them in their car. They tried to fit the rest of the dresser in the back seat of their car but it wouldn't fit. They tried to fit the rest of the dresser in the trunk of their car but it wouldn't fit. They told me that the drawers fit in their car but that the rest of the dresser wouldn't fit in their car. They said they lived close by. They said they didn't know what to do. I told them that the rest of the dresser would probably fit in my car, which was a Subaru, and that I could drive it to their apartment. I went inside and put on my shoes and my hat. I went outside and they had moved the rest of the dresser to my neighbor's driveway behind my neighbor's Subaru. I told them that my Subaru was the other Subaru in the driveway on the other side of the house. They moved the rest of the dresser to the other driveway behind my Subaru. I opened the trunk and moved all the boxes and garbage and umbrellas out of my trunk and into the back seat. They tried to put the rest of the dresser into the trunk of my Subaru but it wouldn't fit. I moved all the boxes and garbage and umbrellas off of the back seat and onto the floor. I lowered one of the back seats all the way. I lowered the other back seat most of the way because of the car seat. I told them that was as far as it would go because of the car seat. They pushed the rest of the dresser onto the back of the half-lowered back seat and shut the trunk. They told me where they lived and how to get there and then drove away in their car. I drove toward where they lived following their directions. There was a major crash at the intersection near where they lived. I sat in traffic while the cops waved at cars and carried pieces of a car bumper around for twenty minutes. I drove past where they lived. I drove to the lake. I opened the trunk of my Subaru. I thought, "This fucking dresser." I pulled the rest of the dresser out of the trunk. I threw the rest of the dresser into the lake. I looked around. I didn't see anyone. I went home. I went to bed.

I'm Here to Commit Some Crimes

I got a new job working at a gas station up the road. It was great. Not really. But kind of. It was good because it was a job. And it even paid slightly better than the grocery store. So it was mostly fine. It was just boring. But that felt okay, because I was boring, too. I was trying to mellow out. I was trying to not punch things anymore. And I was doing pretty okay at it. The guy who trained me at the gas station was named Kramer. On the first day, he showed me how to stock the shelves and count the cigarettes. On the second day, he taught me how to use the register and empty the drawer at night. On the third day, he showed me how to take out the trash by the gas pumps. There was nothing to else to learn after that and he stopped training me and I never saw him again. By then I had some experience letting go of stuff. Nothing ever really happened at the gas station.

But this one day a fifteen-year-old kid came in and asked to buy chewing tobacco. I asked for his ID and he pretended like he didn't hear me. He asked how much the tobacco is. I asked for his ID and he yawned. Like, come on. Come on, kid. I asked for his ID again. He said, "What," and took a twenty-dollar bill out of his pocket. I told him he doesn't look old enough to buy tobacco. He called me a slur and stared at me for a few seconds. The slur didn't make any sense. Or maybe it did, I don't know. Things change over time. Maybe the slur changed. And now I was the slur. Or something.

He left and I watched him get into the passenger seat of a truck. I saw a woman get out of the driver side of the truck. She walked in and asked for three tins of chewing tobacco. I asked her if she's trying to buy tobacco for her fifteen-year-old son. She said, "Yeah." I wasn't sure whether this was illegal or not. She tapped her nails on the counter. She looked at me without saying anything. Her mouth was open. I could see a lot of her teeth. I sold her the tobacco. She left and I watched her hand the tobacco to her son through the window of the truck. Then I stood around for three hours without doing anything. It's hard to explain how my brain felt for three hours alone in the gas station. I guess my brain felt "bad."

A man walked in and he asked if we sold hot dogs. I told him we didn't sell hot dogs. Because we didn't sell hot dogs. He made a face like, "Alright, here goes." He pulled down the waistband of his sweatpants and pulled out his penis. He waggled his penis around with his eyes closed and his tongue sticking out. I looked at his penis. It was really big. It was probably eight or nine inches long. I could hear it flopping against his sweatpants as he waggled it. It seemed flaccid in spite of the size. It sounded like *paff paff paff paff* against his sweatpants. I looked at his hands. He was wearing a wedding ring. That felt good, to me, like someone loved him. I looked at the clock. It was almost time to close the store. I looked back at the man. I looked at his penis. I looked at his face. His face was really funny-looking. Like, he was making a really funny face. He stopped flopping his penis up and down and started spinning it instead. Oh man. He opened his eyes and we made eye contact. He raised his eyebrows. It was still really funny to me. The whole thing. I was laughing a little bit. I couldn't help it. And he laughed, too. It seemed like we were being genuine with each other. Which felt good. I felt like the guy was pretty cool even though he was, like, sexually assaulting me or whatever. He finally put his penis away and pushed over one of those large, cylindrical, free-standing beverage coolers full of energy drinks and ice and it made this huge fucking mess. He ran out of the gas station.

I picked up the energy drinks and put them back into the cooler. I swept up the ice and mopped up the water from the melted ice. No one else came in. I tallied up all the packs and cartons of cigarettes. I paperclipped all the scratch-off lottery ticket receipts. I put the cash into little plastic sheaths and slid them into the safe. I took out the trash by the pumps. I locked the dumpster. I turned on the alarm. I turned off the lights. I drove to my shitty apartment. I lay down on my mattress. I thought about the man who flopped his penis around. I thought about the funny face he made. I thought about the *paff paff paff paff* sound his penis made when he flopped it against his sweatpants. His penis was probably the largest penis I've ever seen in my life. I felt like I had "leveled up," somehow, after seeing it....Does that make sense?

Everything Is Totally Fucked 1

To celebrate that everything was totally fucked, we burned down many things. We burned down the house. We burned down the neighbor's house. We burned down the church. We burned down the other church (cathartic). We burned down the mosque (conflicting). We burned down the diner. We burned down the library. We burned down the tire place (smelled bad). We burned down the athletic center. We burned down the vacant lot (difficult). We burned down the public pool (very difficult). We burned down the woods (easy). We burned down the elementary school. We burned down the grocery store. We burned down the Burger King (mistake). We burned down the music conservatory. We burned down the high school. We burned down the pier. We burned down the middle school. We burned down the candy store. We burned down the hardware store. We burned down the Italian restaurant (smelled good). We burned down the cabinet store. We burned down the other cabinet store. We burned down the other other cabinet store (over on route 42). We burned down the fourth and final cabinet store (success).

Everything Is Totally Fucked 2

To celebrate that everything was totally fucked, I grew out my hair. I cut it off. I grew it out. I cut it off. It kept growing. I kept cutting. It kept growing. A guy I knew in high school ran his car off the road and it burst into flames; he crawled out while on fire and died in the grass between the tree and the road. I don't know where any of my hair went when I cut it off. It's all gone now, probably in a landfill.

Everything Is Totally Fucked 3

To celebrate that everything was totally fucked, I blew some bubbles. The wind carried them off. They went over the ocean. A whale breached the water. A bubble popped in its eye. The soap cleaned all the salt and scum off its eye. The whale saw the unending horizon of the ocean, the endless expanse of flat water and empty sky in all directions. The whale reentered the water. The whale blinked. The whale thought about the endlessness. The whale thought about swimming, breaching, diving, eating, shitting, holding its breath, straining to breach the water to breathe, blowing water out of its blowhole, breathing in air, reentering the water, moving and straining and trying to survive for years and years and years. The whale thought about the ocean, how it never ends, how it continues on in every direction and somehow loops back onto itself. The whale thought about how long life is, about its daily struggle with death, about the pain of every moment, which will pile up into the thing that ultimately kills it, how it will someday be unable to breach the surface of the water and breathe, and how it will eventually die in a protracted agony. The whale ate a moderate amount of plankton and felt tired. The whale breached and looked at the endless expanse of flat water and empty sky in all directions again. The whale felt its vision grow blurry from the salt and dirt and fish shit and scum that floats on the top of the water. I saw a nature documentary once about how large whale penises are—most are larger than I am, sometimes up to ten feet long. I blew some more bubbles. The wind carried them off. I felt, briefly and indignantly, that I had somehow become larger than a whale penis.

Tree

Birds live in the tree behind our shed. All kinds—
blue jays, sparrows, cardinals, robins. They swarm
around during the day. They share the birdbath and
the scattered handfuls of birdseed we throw out into
the grass. They share nests, swapping with the
seasons, sometimes cohabitating—the chickadees
roosting on the nuthatch eggs, the robins feeding the
blue jay chicks, etc. They sing songs together,
squawking, bleeping, loud and annoying. At night
they tell stories—you can see the little bonfires
sparkle through until dawn, and in the morning the
parents leave to go to work. Some work at the
factories near the lake, some at the diners downtown,
some at the elementary school. We watch the baby
chicks grow up and start families and move into new
trees. We watch others enlist in the army, fight in the
war, take selfies with corpses in a burned-out jungle,
come back blind or mutilated or unceasingly angry.
We watch them dig graves, burn bodies, rub blood
on the tree limbs. They build massive edifices of
wicker and bone among the leaves. We hear the
birds cry out at night in agony and fear. They scream
all night—it's terrible, just a horrible noise. My God,
I'm so sick of this fucking tree.

Stretch Your Arms. Stretch Your Fingers. Stretch Your Back. Think About Your Body. Think About Your Body in Freefall. You're Free!

I take a picture of a dog. I send the picture to my husband. My husband takes a picture of a dog. He sends me the picture. We're both near dogs. I could buy an airplane ticket and fly to Nebraska and I could still be near a dog. And most people have ankles. I could send my husband a picture of my ankles, or someone else's ankles, because he likes to think about ankles while he ejaculates, and he likes to ejaculate onto ankles as part of sex. Whenever I want to have sex, I send him a picture of my ankles. Whenever I don't want to have sex, I don't send him a picture of my ankles. I look up the price of plane tickets to Nebraska. I am the only person my husband has ever had sex with. He is the only person to have ejaculated onto my ankles. I buy a plane ticket to Nebraska. I send my husband a picture of my ankles. I get an email receipt for my plane ticket to Nebraska. I look at the receipt and it says, "Debraska." My husband doesn't reply. I don't know where Debraska is. I take a Lyft to the airport. My husband sends me a picture. I don't look at the picture. I fly to Debraska. I hope there are dogs in Debraska.

Today Is Totally Fucked 3

I'm thinking about that scene at the start of *Garden State* where Zach Braff is sitting disaffectedly through a plane crash in slow motion or whatever. I can't believe this is what pops into my head while our plane hits the water. I can't believe this is my last thought. It's so fucking dumb.

Kellogg's Pop-Tarts Frosted S'mores Pastries 2ct

⌒

I felt like shit. I was depressed. I wanted to be shot out of a large gun and into a large bullet shot by another large gun. I closed my laptop. I looked at my hands on my desk. I wanted to strangle my own hands, which didn't make sense. I felt like feeling like shit in a different way. I wanted to explore new ways of feeling like shit, or new types of shit to feel like. I walked to the office kitchen area and swiped my credit card in the vending machine. I pressed the button for a two-pack of Pop-Tarts. The vending machine verified that I could purchase the two-pack of Pop-Tarts for the listed price of $1.25. The two-pack of Pop-Tarts fell halfway down the inside of the machine and got stuck against a protruding Snickers bar. I thought, *The End.* I looked at the two-pack of Pop-Tarts. I looked around the kitchen area of the office. I gently shoved the vending machine. I firmly shoved the vending machine. I punched the vending machine's glass panel. My fist went through the glass panel almost seamlessly; my punch had removed a punch-sized hole in the glass. My hand was maybe four inches away from the two-pack of Pop-Tarts. I heard someone calling my name from somewhere down the hall. I tried moving my hand toward the two-pack of Pop-Tarts. I could feel the edge of the hole in the glass panel start to cut into my skin. It felt really familiar. I didn't scream. I was feeling like shit in the wrong way, or feeling like the wrong kind of shit. I wanted to spend all of my salary on guns for the rest of my life until I died of hunger or a gun accident. I couldn't remember what Pop-Tarts tasted like.

What a Disaster!

I was a bank teller at a bank and one day I forgot why anything mattered and I said, "What a disaster!" I spent ten minutes throwing twenty-dollar bills at the clients until armed security grabbed me and made me pick up all the twenties while they watched angrily and I said, "What a disaster!" I was fired and escorted off of the premises and I said, "What a disaster!"

When I got home, my wife was in bed with another woman, and she told me that I had never adequately fulfilled her in terms of romance, sex, conversation, understanding, and financial security, and I said, "What a disaster!"

She filed for divorce and the judge gave me limited weekend visits with my giant son and I said, "What a disaster!" I spent a year trying to get in shape and improve myself and become a better person so that my family would love me again but instead I put on fifty pounds and got shin splints and I said, "What a disaster!"

I walked in on my son playing with his Legos during one of my limited weekend visits. His mother and her lover were in Naples, drinking wine and making love in the sun. He was building a castle and it was enormous and covered in intricate details. It was the most beautiful castle I had ever seen. I saw in that moment that he was a child imbued with unending potential. I saw in him the beginnings of a world-famous architect worth millions of dollars, able to find and pursue intellectual passions and travel the world and make love to beautiful people in Naples. I walked over to him to kiss him on the head because of how good his Lego castle was but I accidentally kicked the Lego castle and it broke apart and all of its pieces scattered across the floor.

I stepped on all the loose pieces with my bare feet and they all stung the bottoms of my soft, supple feet and I hopped around in pain. My son stood up and punched me in the face. My lip split open and blood came out. My son punched me in the face again and I cried and sobbed silently and blood and drool and tears merged on my swelling face. My son punched me in the face again and I put my hands onto my face and I hunched my shoulders and my body convulsed with pain. My son punched me in the face again and I said, "What a disaster!"

My son sat down and started playing with his Legos. I watched him rebuild the castle. It was identical to the first castle. It was perfect.

Taking even just 5 minutes to sit quietly and follow your breath can help you feel more conscious and connected for the rest of your day

Post-assembly-line world. Mickey Mouse with a fat dick world. Something something world. The president ran out of excuses so he just started telling the truth and everyone forgot to care and hell yeah. I was lucky because I was the president at the time. I kept a bear on the grounds and he killed the ambassador to Slovenia. I tweeted out a picture of Mickey Mouse fisting Goofy's asshole when people asked about it and the picture got entered into the presidential records library. Someone tried to shoot down Air Force One so I had sex with my wife on national TV. Fuck you. Someone made a mashup video of me fucking my wife in the Oval Office and the bear killing the ambassador to Slovenia. It's hard to watch: me fucking my wife, the bear ripping out the ambassador's organs, me cumming deep in my wife's pussy, the bear facing the camera with blood on its muzzle, me pulling out and getting sauce everywhere (I call cum "sauce" and I talk about cum a lot during my press conferences so it's like a thing). Someone on the internet said we could pack it up,

America was over, and I retweeted that because I agreed, I thought the country was a fucking trash pit and I hated my job and all the people in the world. The video kicks ass. The video also went into the presidential library or whatever. It's, like, damn, seems bad but also kinda good. People started calling cum "sauce" after the video came out. I will continue to have sex with my wife on TV, too. Disney really put out an animated porno thing about Mickey Mouse fisting Goofy's asshole after all that. It's official. We're running out of ideas or something. Someone said that, someone said something like: there's nothing left to manufacture. I think that's a Chomsky thing, I think he said something like that originally, but he's dead now. I'm cumming deep in my wife's pussy again. There it goes, there goes the sauce, baby. We're on camera. Check out this sauce, motherfuckers. I'm the sauce master. President Saucemaster. I feel suicidal every day and I don't know how anyone doesn't feel this way.

Today Is Totally Fucked 4

I drive to the grocery store. I buy groceries. I drive home. I put the groceries away. I go out onto the fire escape. I think about how many more times I will need to drive to the grocery store and buy groceries and drive home in my life. I think about how many more times I will go out onto the fire escape and think about how many more times I will need to drive to the grocery store and buy groceries and drive home in my life, etc. etc. etc.

When I go to sleep, I think about putting wooden train tracks together. When I wake up, I think about cooking breakfast. I don't know what I think about in between. No, just kidding. I think I will drive my car off the road without noticing. I will spend several hours thinking about the best way to spell the sound of the car crash, and I won't ever know how to spell it right, and then I'll be dead. No, I don't know. I don't know what's wrong with me. Everything is totally fine.

I go stay at my parents' house for a few days. We eat pizza and watch TV. The pizza is called "garbage pizza" because of all the toppings. My parents get into an argument about health insurance. I lie on the bed in the guest room and I text my sister. I ask her how she wants to die and she responds that she wants to be *fucked to death*. I go to sleep thinking about putting wooden train tracks together. I wake up and I think about cooking breakfast.

I cook breakfast and I imagine my sister's funeral, where above her coffin is a blue and yellow banner that says: *Fucked to Death,* and my parents are still arguing about health insurance, and I spend several hours thinking about the best way to spell the sound of the car crash, but I won't ever know how to spell it right. That feels right, I think. That feels like how her funeral will be. I text her this and she agrees. She sends me a thumbs up emoji. I text her to ask if she'll be coming to Mom and Dad's today, but she doesn't reply.

Dog in the World

I made a car out of cardboard. I put the dog into the car. The dog drove away. She never came back, but I assume she is okay, based on what I know about the dog. She's a good dog.

Happy and Content and Slowly Teaching Yourself How to Eat Glass

I'm at work. I'm trying to convert a file from one file format to another file format. I'm not sure how to do it. I try renaming the file manually but the program that needs the file to be in this new format doesn't recognize it as a valid file of that format. I am looking this up online. I use the search engine that everyone uses. Some of the links are advertisements for software that can convert files and costs $59.95. Some of the links are for blogs designed to sell copies of self-help ebooks. I keep thinking, "Converting files" over and over again while scrolling and clicking on links. I click the little *x* in various advertisements and pop-ups about cookies and pop-ups about installing applications and pop-ups about getting updates and pop-ups about signing up for newsletters and pop-ups about subscribing to online machine-learning classes. I think, "Converting files." I spend seven hours scrolling and clicking and thinking, "Converting files." A man walks up to my desk and asks if I'm busy. I'm sweating and I'm very thirsty. I clear my throat and tell him I'm busy. I point at my computer screen without looking at him. I don't recognize his voice. My eyes are kind of unfocused. I think, "Converting files." I click on a link and it prompts me to upload my file. The man asks me what I'm doing. I click the file upload button while thinking, "Converting files." The file browser opens up and I navigate to the file. The man walks closer. I'm still pointing at the screen. I think, "Converting files" while selecting the file. I click the wrong file. I can't see that well. My eyes hurt. The man is closer. I'm sweating. I'm thinking, "Converting files." My finger is touching the screen. The man is next to me. I think, "Converting files." I click on a button that says, "Select." The man is sweating. The man is whispering something. I think, "Converting files." My finger is bent from the force of pressing on the screen. I click "Convert file." The blood is draining from my finger. I think, "Converting files." The man whispers, "Converting files." I look at my finger. It looks like a sixth finger, like my hand has six fingers, or like my hand has a penis, and, for a second, I think, "Penis fingers." The website says, "Converting file(s)."

The Wall Is a Mirror that Shows You What You'd Look Like if You Were a Wall

⌒

I'm sitting in the passenger seat of Darien's shitty 2003 Aztek. I'm holding the pizzas we have to deliver. Darien asks if I like metal and I don't say anything because I don't like metal but Darien is training me on delivering pizzas and I don't want him to dislike me. Darien puts on some metal and drinks two tiny bottles of Hot Damn. The pizzas are warm in my lap. I think about my penis being warmed by the pizzas while Darien puts the car into reverse. He peels out over the gravel behind the pizza place, arcing us backwards while staring straight through the windshield. He puts the car into drive and looks at the pizzas in my lap for two or three seconds. I look at him looking at the pizzas. He puts the car into drive and drives us through the alley and hits one of the metal trash cans. I hear him talking to himself as if he's talking to someone else. I think about a Zachary German story I read the night before. In the story, a character named Zachary German spends four hours alone in a cafe drinking coffee and looking at social media on his phone. He slips on some ice on his way to the car afterwards and lands on his ass. He thinks, "Bitch, I'll fucking kill you." He drives home while listening to a local radio station. He goes into his apartment and sees his wife and child playing with a bunch of plastic bullshit. He looks at the plastic bullshit and thinks, "Bitch, I'll fucking kill you." Zachary German and his wife and child each eat some ham cubes at the dining room table. He tells his wife that he wrote four thousand words at the cafe and that he felt good about what he wrote but that he would probably cut a good portion of it later. He throws the leftover ham cubes away and looks at the ham cubes in the trash can and thinks, "Bitch, I'll fucking kill you." They leave the apartment and drive to a music class for toddlers. In the music class for toddlers, Zachary German dances enthusiastically as part of a large circle of parents also dancing enthusiastically. He looks at himself dancing in a mirror placed against the wall and thinks, "Bitch, I'll fucking kill you." During the part of the music class for toddlers where all the toddlers get to play with tambourines, he sits on a chair and feels a strong desire to smoke a cigarette or walk through a thunderstorm while crying uncontrollably and thinks, "Bitch, I'll fucking kill you." During the part of the music class for toddlers where everyone lies down in the dark and sings quietly, he thinks about how much he likes ham cubes and thinks, "Bitch, I'll fucking kill you." Later that night, in bed, after making love to his wife, Zachary German thinks about having sex with a pizza. I stop thinking about the story because that's where the story ends. Darien's still mumbling to himself. I feel like I might get decapitated by a semi-truck tire rupturing on the highway. Darien narrows his eyes and points through the windshield like he's trying to start shit with someone. Darien says, "Hey man, you're eating a *dick* pizza, man."

I Am Going to Burn Down the Mall of America

⁓

We're at this place. It's next to the pizza place, the new one with the cheap pizza, and it's by the party store, the one with the snacks and beer and wine but no liquor. We should have gone to that one to buy forties, for the snacks, but they have worse forties, because they sell underage, and we're old enough to buy, so we buy at the liquor store, but it's stupid, because there's no food or anything. Whatever. We pick out some 40oz bottles of malt liquor. We do math in our heads about the forties and the time it takes to bake a pizza, because there's the pizza place. We should buy liquor, maybe, but we don't want liquor. We can just have the forties. But they take time to drink, and you don't want to walk around with an open forty, but you could, and we have to walk to our apartment anyway, but we don't want to go back yet. I think that we could drink the forties in the bathroom of the pizza place but then we'd want another forty after. Or we could drink them in the normal area of the pizza place because it's new and they don't care, just like the party store, like, they'd be fine with whatever. This whole block has that vibe. Except the liquor store, which is weird, but whatever. We go back to the refrigerator area. We don't know how to spell refrigerator. We talk about it a little bit.

It's pretty funny. They have twenty-twos of stuff, which we could drink faster, but it's not a good deal, and we'd rather get two forties than four twenty-twos. You call out to the cashier and ask which beer is best to drink in a bathroom but he just gives a thumbs up, which isn't helping anything, but it's helping the mood, which I guess is something, which is good, yeah. Feels like we can do this. The vibe of the liquor store is pretty good now. That guy's pretty cool. We don't feel like figuring this out yet. We're shuffling bottles around, fogging up the fridge doors. It smells like damp cardboard. We're squatting behind the racks of wine, secretly drinking your forty.

Going Out

I got some blood drawn. I felt tingly and weird. I told the phlebomimist I was feeling faint. and She breathed in. She said, "Okay." She seemed disapointd. I was feeling hot and cold at the same time, like cold in some zones and hot with thee other ones. She asked if I was feling hot or cold. I said I was feeling all of them. She said, "Okay." She sighed while looking at me. She walked o ver the door and said, "Alex! Hey alex, we need, we got, uh." She looked at me. I felt like I was suppposed to [ut my head between my knees bu she didn't seem to thinkg I should based on not teooing me to. She said, "Alejandro! Alejandro we have, uh, he's feeling fdaint." I liked Alejandro. He drew my blood lasttime and I din't feel faint when he did it. He had a good ssmile. When I siged the forms for the bloodd thing it says, "Have youever felt faint from giving blood drawn" and I checked "no " because it was. Alejandro came in.He wasn't smiling. He tried to push a special chsair through the doorway but t wouldn't fit. He pulled it back outtof the doorway. I was feeling sweaey and cold and generally pretty shitty. Alejandro came In and they both helf my arms and walked me trhouygh the doorway and to the reclining shair. The phlbemosnits asked if I wantedany apple juice or something. she didn't specify the something but I didn't reallyw ant apple juice. I thinmk I would have preferred cranberry juice. I thiughot about telling her about how once when I was a kid my family ata e a restaurant and the ewaiter asked if I wanetd a fruit juice nad I said yes and aksed what kinds she had and she said "any kind of juice" and so I said "raspverry" and she frowned nd said "not reapsberyy." I had the applejuice and dr ank it really fast and the pjhlebondxmsist said wow you drank that fas"t and I felt self sconsous in a new way, on top of all th ways I weas feeling self consosucu already . Im tryng really hard to get this fall down before I pass out sory I"ll be home sooni think

Holding Your Breath So You Don't Have to Breathe So Much Sometimes

⌒

I was in Montana, driving down the highway. There were those concrete median things on both sides. The shoulders disappeared so I had to drive carefully, close to the concrete things. Then it went from four lanes to three lanes to two lanes and then finally one lane. I was the only car going east as far as I could see. The concrete median things crept closer and closer. I had to slow down. The road was pretty narrow. I felt like I was almost through, like I just had to drive a little bit more and then things would open up again, so I drove very slowly and with a great deal of concentration. I leaned forward with my eyes wide open. I turned off the music. But I started bumping into the medians. Just a little bit. And, each time, I'd jerk the wheel to correct, but then bump the other median, and do it again, back and forth. I felt okay about it, though. I felt like there was nothing else I could do. I was doing my best trying to make it through. It didn't feel like my fault. I imagined reasoning with a judge in traffic court, saying, *The road just got so narrow, I figured whoever put the medians up should have known this was inevitable and then they should have done something to prevent it.* I imagined the judge agreeing with me. I drove slower and slower as the medians got tighter and tighter. Eventually the medians narrowed enough that they were constantly scraping the sides of the car. I thought I just had a little bit farther to go, so I kept going. It seemed like it would end up fine because none of this was my fault and I figured that paint is just paint, or whatever, and I could get the car fixed. I had some money saved up. I also didn't care about the car, really. But eventually the car got completely stuck, wedged between the two medians. I couldn't go forward. I couldn't back up. I looked in the rear-view mirror and didn't see any cars coming. I turned off the car. I imagined stupidly explaining to the tow truck guy that I thought it was going to be fine so I just kept driving. I climbed out of the sunroof and sat on the top of the car. I looked out and saw the medians merging into a nubby triangle of concrete that poked out over a flat, endless expanse of blue ocean. I was so fucking mad.

Today Is Totally Fucked 1

I woke up. I thought about the day. I thought about giving up. I gave up. I stayed in bed. The bed sprouted legs. The bed broke through the wall. The load-bearing beams developed hairline cracks. The plaster was everywhere. I was awake. I hated it. I coughed. The bed shushed me. The bed carried me into the yard. The grass pulled itself out of the ground. The dirt moved itself aside. The bed dumped me into the hole. There was dirt and blankets and plaster everywhere. I was lying in the hole at a really weird angle. The dirt poured itself over me and filled the hole. The grass replanted itself. The bed slumped over near the house and turned into garbage. The house started to crumble and turned into garbage. It rained. The bed turned into wet garbage. The house turned into wet garbage. I stayed in the ground. The water soaked into the ground. I turned into wet garbage. Nothing really happened after that.

Everything Is

Totally Fine

Freedom Is an Abstract Entity That Interacts with The World in Concrete Ways

e

A mouse climbed onto the top of a man's head. The mouse pulled the man's hair and controlled him like a puppet. The mouse made the man apply for a good job. The mouse made the man work 9-6 every weekday for ten years. The mouse made the man start a Roth IRA and invest in his 401k. The mouse made the man buy ingredients in bulk and cook food. The mouse made the man go to an open house in a neighborhood with low property values but a burgeoning commercial area and convenient access to the highway. The mouse made the man put in an offer on the house. The mouse made the man invest in solar panels and good windows. The mouse made the man replace the lawn with regionally appropriate and biodiverse flora. The mouse made the man work out every day. The mouse made the man get into collecting coins. The mouse made the man call his parents twice a week. The mouse made the man go on dates. The mouse made the man marry a wonderful person. The mouse made the man have children. The mouse made the man take his family camping. The mouse made the man take up stamp collecting. The mouse made the man invest in the stock market. The mouse made the man encourage his children to pursue their dreams. The mouse made the man set up a good life insurance plan. The mouse made the man transition into consulting work to spend more time with his family. The mouse made the man take classes at the adult learning annex. The mouse made the man retire early and travel with his wife after the kids graduated college. The mouse made the man look up at the stars at night. The mouse made the man spend time in nature. The mouse made the man kiss his wife every night before bed. The mouse made the man tell her that he loved her. The mouse made the man close his eyes and go to sleep.

Bright Future

❧

Barack Obama put a bag of red lentils and a chopped onion and a bay leaf into the crockpot and turned it on low for six to eight hours. He turned off the crockpot and took out the bay leaf and ate the lentils while watching the public access channel. He called his girlfriend long distance but she didn't answer. He washed the crockpot and bowl and spoon and lay on his mattress. He smoked a cigarette and thought about being a famous author. He thought about being president. He thought about moving to Montana and opening an organic food cooperative; he imagined himself shooting a rifle in a big empty field at a cardboard cutout, smoking cigarettes and drinking beer. He stood up and looked through his dresser for clothes he didn't need anymore and put them in a bag by the front door of his apartment.

He sat at his typewriter and wrote a story: *I will rip out your teeth! I will rip out my teeth! I will shuffle our teeth together like cards! Like a deck of playing cards! The shuffling will make a special sound! That sound will be the sound of my love for you! We're going to the beach! I will throw you into the surf! I will fish you out with a fishing pole! You will flap your arms like fins! Above the water! I will reel you in! I will put you into a bucket of water! You will bleed in the water and you will die in the bucket! I will take you home and put you to bed! And we will do it again* the next day! I will break into your dad's house! I will pretend to be your mom! Your dad will kiss me on the lips! I will kiss him back! I will cook him dinner! He will grout the tile in the upstairs bathroom! I will call you on the phone! I will tell you I love you! And I will eat cookies in bed! And I will watch cable TV with your dad! And I will go to sleep without brushing my teeth! And your dad will try to kiss me again! And I won't kiss him back! And your dad will get the hint! And your dad will roll over and face the wall! And I will roll over and face the other wall! And I won't have sex with your dad! And I will leave in the middle of the night! You will give me all of your laundry! And I won't do your laundry! I'll just leave it at the laundromat! I'll disappear! You'll never hear from me again! I'll be gone! You will have to get your laundry on your own! Years will go by! You will try to look me up in the phone book! But eventually you'll move on! You'll fall in love with someone else! That person will do your laundry! That person won't disappear! That person won't break into your dad's house! That person won't fish you out of the ocean! That person won't rip out your teeth! You'll be so happy! For years! And when you die, you won't remember me!

He looked at the story and corrected typos with a fine-tipped blue pen while smoking a cigarette. He tried calling his girlfriend again. He sat at his desk and thought about his father's death, about what it'd feel like to die in a car crash, about how he'd probably die before anything good could ever happen again. He turned off the desk lamp and lay in bed. He thought about what he could do to improve the story he was working on. He masturbated to a memory of his fifth-grade math teacher and when he finished, he realized he couldn't remember her name.

White Zinfandel 1

&

Greg bought a bottle of white zinfandel and a six pack of hard cider to split with his old high school friends who were visiting for the weekend, who said they would drink with him but who then decided they didn't want to drink and insisted instead that Greg do all the drinking, so they could see him get drunk, which they said seemed "just as good" as getting drunk themselves for the first time, which was originally the plan, so Greg started drinking the white zinfandel and put on the first DVD of the Simpsons Season 8 and opened a bag of $2 Cheeto puff snack things from the party store.

His friends had an intense conversation about the construction and design of the dorm room—the positioning of the heat vent relative to the window, the color of the walls, the light fixture in the bathroom, and the quality and color of the carpet—and the cheap furniture and decorations—the plastic lamps and futon that Greg had purchased from Walmart, the movie posters he bought from the campus book store, the empty beer and wine bottles he had collected on the bookshelf—and the generally poor upkeep of the room—the overflowing laundry bin in the open closet area, the pubic hair on and around the toilet, the layer crumbs and food wrappers on and around the futon—as part of a larger argument about where they each would sleep.

Greg continued to drink the white zinfandel at a rate he lost track of because of a desire to get as drunk as possible as quickly as possible, feeling optimistic that by drinking both heavily and quickly he would be able to instantiate the excitement that his friends expected his drinking to bring to the weekend—he envisioned himself becoming drunk and powerful and carefree and leading his friends through some kind of mixed indoor/outdoor adventure that would, in spite of their original and immediately negative opinions about his dorm room, foster in his friends' minds a sense of awe and respect for his new semi-adult life away at college, living in a dorm, surrounded by other barely-adults with free time and alcohol and snacks and open green spaces and a moderately interesting downtown area close to campus.

He finished drinking the white zinfandel before the end of the first episode.

His friends were still talking about his shitty dorm room.

He left the dorm room and walked down the hallway and through the double-wide doors and down the concrete steps and up to the bike rack where he unlocked his bike and got on his bike and rode toward downtown and blacked out.

The Novelist

He sits down at his laptop. He's thirsty. He wants to write. He has music stuck in his head. He's writing something. The song stuck in his head is about a dog and a cat. He thinks about how he's thirsty. He thinks he should give up on all things, just completely abandon himself to the whims of the universe and die in a field. He thinks about wanting to write. The music stuck in his head is a kid's song. *I have a dog his name is Christopher Alex James and he is a happy puppy dog (arf! arf!).* His wrist hurts. He's writing about pizza. None of this feels worth it. He wonders when his arm will no longer be useful. He thinks about how his wife used to clean a house for someone who was a musician but who fucked up her arm and she couldn't do anything anymore, and that was why she hired his wife to clean her house and stuff. He imagines a day when his arm won't work and he won't be able to work and he'll die without any money. *I have a cat her name is Melissa Agnes Jane she's really a silly cat I never know where she's at (mreeow!).* He thinks about the amount of work it will take to write another novel. He thinks about how his dad used to tell him to wear a helmet when he rode his bike because his brain was the only way he'd get himself a good job. He writes something about pizza. He thinks about how his daughter might grow up a complete stranger and he'll never know what he did wrong. *Meow meow meow meowww meow meow meow! Arf! Arf!*

Roof

Alex went to a party at Brian's. After everyone else left, Alex and Brian sat on the roof eating pizza and drinking Guinness. It was the first college party Alex ever went to.

Brian started talking about how in love he was. He was so in love, he said. But she didn't love him back, he said. Alex asked who Brian was talking about. Brian said a name that didn't sound like a name. Brian said that being in love was horrible. He said it was the worst thing anyone could ever do. He told Alex to never fall in love.

Alex had never been in love before. Alex had never been drunk before. Alex had never eaten pizza on a roof before. Alex had never listened to someone talk about being in love before. Everything felt new and insane in a good way.

Alex threw pizza crusts into the street. Brian lay down on the roof and sighed. He asked Alex if he was in love with anyone. Alex said he wasn't sure. Brian said that love is a choice and that he had made the wrong one. Brian said that he should never have fallen in love. He asked Alex if he knew what he meant. Alex watched a car run over the pizza crusts he had thrown onto the street. Brian asked Alex if he knew what he was saying. He was slurring his words really badly. Alex made a noncommittal hand motion. He didn't know what Brian was saying but he wanted Brian to keep talking.

Brian said that love was always the wrong choice to make, that the problem with people is that they are constantly making choices, and thus constantly making the wrong choices, and thus constantly creating pain for themselves and others. He said that love was always the wrong thing to pursue, that love would destroy all other feelings.

He said that love was a failure to reason, that loving someone meant that you were wrong, fundamentally wrong, that you misjudged the universe and your own sense of purpose. He said that any person who chose to be in love was *defective*. He said that being in love was proof you had *brain damage*. He said that being in love was *simply wrong*, that it was *aberrant*. He said that choosing to love was *choosing defeat*, that choosing love was *accepting death*. He said that life is an accumulation of choices and outcomes and that choosing love, ever, even a single time, meant that you had failed, that your life would forever be *lesser*, would be *marred* by your own idiocy. He said that his life was thus *broken*, that he had a *broken life*, that his accomplishments would *come up short*, that anyone who chose to reject love would inevitably be *one step ahead*. He said that he chose to be a *failure* because of love. Then he fell asleep on the roof.

Alex threw an empty bottle into the street and was disappointed in the small sound it made. Nothing happened. The bottle was gone in the darkness. Brian was snoring. Alex felt alone. Alex left and rode his bike down the unlit streets back to campus.

He had never ridden a bike at four in the morning before. He had never left a drunk person sleeping on a roof before. He had never thrown a bottle into the street before. He had never heard a really drunk person talk about love before. Everything continued to feel new and insane in a good way.

Alex was drunk. He climbed into a bunk bed while drunk. He crawled out of a bunk bed while drunk. He walked to the bathroom. He peed in the sink. He peed in the sink while flipping off the mirror. He tilted his penis up to hit the mirror with pee. He let go of his penis so he could flip off the mirror with both hands. He said, "Fuck you" really quietly with his eyes closed while still flipping off the mirror with both hands and peeing in the sink.

The rim of the sink was cold on his penis. Alex thought about Brian sleeping on the roof. He thought about love. He thought about Brian. He thought about how good peeing was. He thought about how he wished he could pee forever while flipping off the mirror with both hands.

The Anxious Personal Trainer

He holds a plank and thinks about how much he will suffer when his dog passes away. He thinks about how he will fill the loss with comfort food and prolonged dormancy. He thinks about how many more planks he will need to hold to rebuild the atrophied muscle. He counts to ten and switches positions. He looks at his dog and recognizes his life as an accumulation of protracted effort and inevitable decay.

Basketball Men

❧

There was a man and he was named Douglas, and he had a cellphone with applications installed on it. The applications showed him content that he often despaired over for hours on end. When he coughed, it scared his dogs, and they hid under the bed. When his wife came home from work, she sighed deeply while looking at him and left to take a shower.

Douglas liked to imagine himself a basketball man, one of the guys on the courts, who could hoop balls with ease and frivolity. Every basketball man had over a million dollars, used the cell phone applications in an evocative and irreverent way, and drove a large car with no care for the cost of gasoline. Every basketball man went to interesting parties, as well, and was in a loving, sustaining relationship with someone for whom love came easily and thoroughly.

The day his wife didn't come home after work was like every other day. Douglas used his cell phone to look up basketball men. He used his cell phone to look up fifty-day cardio workout regimens. He used his cell phone to read about war crimes; the country he lived in was using its military to commit war crimes. "We're going to commit war crimes," the president had said, and then, after some bombs blew up somewhere, the president said, "We did it, and doing it kicked ass." Douglas texted his wife and she texted back that she had found a new life to live.

Things happened in the world and the people in the world continued to grapple with these things in frustratingly ineffective ways. Douglas woke up every morning with the realization that he was alive until he wouldn't be, and every evening he forgot. He practiced throwing a ball into a hoop. He understood that people were in charge or they weren't, or something. They eventually put lead back into gasoline. They made suicide illegal. They stopped paying the basketball men so much money to do dunks, and the sport fell into disarray, so Douglas stopped working on his dunks. His wife eventually came home, too, and acted like nothing had happened.

They also redefined what a war crime was so that people wouldn't worry so much, and people stopped worrying so much. It was good.

The First Millennial President

The first millennial president spaces out. She's looking at a Word document. But not really looking. Seems like too much to care about. And there are other people being paid to do it in case she doesn't feel like it. So she's not sure what she's supposed to be doing. It feels like studying for a shitty test. She feels bad.

She thinks about how you can do anything you want in the oval office. She thinks about killing herself in the oval office. She thinks maybe that would be good. She listens to Pedro the Lion's last album, the one they put out after David Bazan—the only consistent member of the band—killed himself. Every song on the album is about wanting to kill himself. The last song on the album is about deciding to actually kill himself. She likes that the last song ends with him saying, "Oh my God" maybe a foot away from the microphone and putting his guitar down. You can hear it thunk against a wooden floor or something. It feels relatable.

One of the songs on the last Pedro the Lion album has a line in it that compares his divorce to being the president: "When things end like this / you convince yourself it's useless / I think how lonely it must be / being president of the land of the free / one nation under God / who, by the way, is dead."

She closes her laptop and goes to the bathroom. She pees, washes her hands, takes three THC tablets, and breaks open her safety razor. She takes the razor blade to the rooftop garden. The secret service guys nod. One of them points to the moon—it's huge and low against the horizon.

She thinks about how someone at a campaign rally meet-and-greet thing for her second presidential run asked her to send someone to the moon again. He asked her why she was being such a pussy about the moon thing. She asked him if he wanted to go.

"Do you want to go? You can go. We can do it." The guy looked worried and didn't say anything. She shook his hand and smiled and leaned in close and said, "I'll put you on the fucking moon and leave you there, you worthless piece of shit." Someone caught it on tape and it became a whole thing. Her mother died the week she was inaugurated and at the funeral someone asked her about the moon thing and she started laughing because of how insane it all was.

She thinks about how stupid she feels and throws the safety razor blade into the garden below. She flips off the moon and laughs. One of the secret service guys laugh, too, but she's unsure why.

White Zinfandel 2

⌒

He woke up on a large flat boulder near the river. The sun was just barely rising over the water. He was covered in morning dew and vomit mixed with popcorn. His mouth tasted like vomit mixed with popcorn. The boulder was covered in vomit mixed with popcorn. Little birds were flitting about on the boulder, pecking at the vomit mixed with popcorn.

Hold Music

ᗡ

Greg ordered a pizza. The pizza had a suicide note in the box, lying loose on top of the pizza. It was signed by someone else named Greg. Greg called the pizza place but the connection was bad. He tried to tell the guy that there was a suicide note in his pizza box but the guy thought Greg was trying to place an order. Greg kept saying, "No, no, listen," but the guy sounded really distracted and mad. Greg looked at the clock and saw that it was probably really busy at the pizza place. The guy asked Greg how many orders of breadsticks he wanted. Greg hung up and called back but the line was busy. He hung up and called back and the guy answered and put him on hold. Greg listened to hold music while rereading the suicide note. The Greg who wrote the suicide note felt deeply concerned for his girlfriend. He speculated that she would not handle his death well. The Greg who wrote the suicide note was trying to ask the pizza place to give his girlfriend money to help her deal with the aftermath of his suicide. Greg wondered about the kind of relationship this other Greg had with the pizza place. He wondered how the note had ended up in his pizza box. He listened to the hold music. He read the suicide note again. He liked how the Greg who wrote the suicide note sketched out how exactly he planned on killing himself, which didn't seem normal for suicide notes because the people who find them usually also find the body. He ate a slice of the pizza while listening to the hold music and rereading the suicide note. The music was pretty good. It was classic hip-hop. He thought maybe using classic hip-hop for hold music was illegal somehow—he couldn't think of any other reason other places would use generic hold music instead of classic hip-hop. He also thought about how he liked how the Greg who wrote the suicide note wrote *f* and *t* with a squiggle for the little crossbar thing instead of just a straight line.

The Man and His Toddler and the Woman Doing Some Kind of Workout Routine

The man stood in the baseball diamond while his toddler examined an anthill. The ants were digging new tunnels or looking for food or whatever. The man stood up straight and looked around. It was sunny. The air was good. The baseball diamond was next to a large grassy field. There were some tennis courts and trees and a walking path and a road with cars on it. There weren't many people out because it was like three in the afternoon on a weekday. There was a woman doing some kind of workout routine near the bleachers. The man looked at the clouds. He considered looking at his phone. His toddler destroyed an anthill and dug in the loose dirt near the edge of the baseball diamond. The man looked at the woman doing pushups or something with her hands on the bottom bleacher and her feet on the ground. The man talked to his toddler about the ants. He told the toddler that the ants were black and they had six legs and lived in tunnels underground. His toddler made an excited noise and started picking some small white flowers near the edge of the baseball diamond. The man watched a car drive by. He looked at the woman doing crunches in the grass. His toddler asked to be picked up. He held onto his toddler's hands and let his toddler climb up his legs and stomach and into his arms. His toddler pointed to another edge of the baseball diamond where there were dandelions. The man carried his toddler to the dandelions. He talked to his toddler about how the sky was blue and the clouds were white and the dirt was brown. The man set his toddler down. He looked at the woman lying on the ground with her legs and arms spread out. He crouched down and looked at the dandelions. He talked about the dandelions while his toddler ripped one apart. His toddler picked and then threw all the remaining dandelions one by one into the dirt and asked to be picked up again. His toddler pointed to the pitcher's mound. He carried his toddler to the pitcher's mound and said, "Ready! Set! Go!" and his toddler ran from the top of the mound toward home base for about ten feet, then walked back to the top of the mound. They did this again three or four times until his toddler got distracted by a small hole in the dirt. The man looked at the woman continuing to lie flat in the grass. The man looked at his phone. He thought about how much time it'd take to walk home and how much time it'd take to cook dinner. He thought about cooking dinner every night except for Friday night for an indefinitely long time, probably decades. He liked cooking dinner. He picked up his toddler and walked to the edge of the baseball diamond toward the dandelions. He held his toddler low to the ground so his toddler could pick a dandelion to carry home. He looked at the woman lying, unmoving, in the grass. He carried his toddler down the walking path to the road, crossed the road, and walked down the sidewalk to his apartment, which was across the street from the baseball diamond. He carried his toddler inside and took off their shoes. His toddler placed the dandelion on the bookcase and drank from a water bottle. The man sat on the couch and looked through the front window. He looked at the woman lying in the grass. She propped herself up on her elbows and looked at her watch. The man lay down on the couch and felt like a dumbass.

You Don't Have to Say You Love Me

❧

She often felt dispassionate in a general, amorphous way, toward—and about—everything. She felt no deeply personal connection with her husband, who, she imagined, felt the same way. She felt unguilty about her apathy toward him and their relationship, which she imagined both of them understood and accepted as mutual, nondefining, reasonable, etc.

She recorded a video of herself singing a pop song on her living room couch. She watched the video several times. She tried to determine whether she sang anything completely wrong or looked particularly ugly. She felt that the video was good. She put a black and white filter on the video. She posted the video to Facebook.

She saw that several family members and acquaintances commented on the video with supportive comments and heart emojis. She replied to each one to point out what she felt was the most relevant flaw in her appearance or performance.

She felt conflicted about the video. She thought about how her family and acquaintances reacted to it. She thought about emojis, how they worked, and how anyone knew how they worked, which seemed like an impossible-to-answer question. She saw that the video had been viewed two hundred times. She imagined herself forty years in the future, having entirely forgotten about the video and almost every other aspect of her current life.

She looked at things on the internet. She brushed her teeth. She went to bed and initiated sex with her husband. She held him close against her body after he ejaculated. She focused on the feeling of his penis shrinking while inside her. She felt, briefly and intensely, as if his penis were *decaying* inside her, and gasped audibly.

The Only Good Car

The car doesn't have a radio anymore. The tires are loose. The windshield is missing. It barely has any windows at all. The roof is too small. The trunk is nailed shut. The seats rotate freely. At night, it sleeps with its mouth open and snores. But he doesn't mind, because it's the only good car.

Giving Up Requires Agency in a Way that Feels Like It Shouldn't by Virtue of Being the Act of Giving Up

❧

The man got drunk. He blacked out. He drove toward home. He ran over a stop sign. He woke up in jail. He had dried blood on his arms and face. He went home. He poured out all of the beer in his fridge. He went to court. He paid for a new stop sign. He took the bus to work. He called people and asked them for forgiveness. He got his license back. He had a breathalyzer machine installed in his car. He drove carefully. He drank iced tea. He talked to a judge. He had the breathalyzer machine removed from his car. He cut down the stop sign with a hacksaw. He put the stop sign in the back of his car. He drove around for a while. He drove to a public park. He took out the stop sign and tried to throw it like a Frisbee, but the stump of the stick thing cut his arm and he shouted "fuck" really loudly. The stop sign landed maybe four feet away. He felt miserable in a deep, ominous way.

Leap of Faith

༂

There was a really bad month where every night Billy stayed up late after his wife went to bed. He would listen to podcasts and play a skateboarding video game. He had vague memories of how it all worked from when he played it as a kid—all the best combos, unlocking all the secret areas, getting high scores. He'd spend two to five hours doing kickflips and darkslides in places he'd never been to, like Tokyo or California, while listening to men from New Zealand talk about movies he'd never seen.

One of these nights he paused the game and stared at the TV screen because everything felt extra bad and different. When he was in eighth grade he went to a church camp. At the end, the youth pastors sat him in a room and asked if he believed in Jesus. He panicked, feeling overwhelmed by what was happening, and he saw their heads grow grotesquely huge, as if he was seeing, for the first time, what the world around him truly looked like without the leveling filter of experience and expectation. He was thirsty, hot, sweaty, cold, and his eyesight went grey and swirly. The youth pastors were flopping balloons, or horrible oil paintings of flopping balloons. He stammered through a non-answer about Jesus so he could leave, to be free of what was happening. He felt that way again, staring at the TV screen. He felt fully detached from himself. He thought, "Whoever this person is, he is doing a bad job, he shouldn't be playing this videogame, he shouldn't be ignoring his obligations, he shouldn't be doing what he's doing at all, but he's still doing it even though he should stop."

He often used a cell phone application called Twitter to view and recommend to others a diverse array of ironic, cynical, sarcastically violent, earnestly violent, and/or politically extreme media that leveraged characters and stylistic themes/imagery from Japanese animation, low-resolution still shots and promotional material from outdated computer games, and assorted iconography, turns of phrase, and/or images appropriated from disparate internet communities of which he was not a member. But he also used the cell phone application to communicate his earnest thoughts and feelings so that people on the internet could console him in his depression or talk him down during bad episodes of anxiety.

He tweeted about how he felt this strange detachment and someone sent him a Twitter direct message saying that he was probably having a dissociative episode and that even though it happens to people sometimes, he shouldn't tweet about it, because of how employers and family and whoever else can see his tweets and might do something that would make his life worse, like send him to a psychiatric hospital or prevent him from getting a different job. He thanked the person, deleted the tweet, and read most of the "Dissociative disorder" article on Wikipedia.

He unpaused the skateboarding game. He disassociated some more. He had a hard time playing the game but liked having a word for what was happening. He paused the game. He looked at Twitter. He saw a brand entity icon account post a joke about video games. Billy replied to the brand entity icon account's post with a death threat. The brand entity icon account was verified on Twitter. Billy looked up how to be verified on Twitter. The verification process required a photo identification and filling out bureaucratic-seeming forms; it didn't seem to make any sense for a brand to be verified on Twitter. Billy deleted his death threat and then tweeted at the brand entity icon account to ask if it had photo identification. The brand entity icon account quote-tweeted Billy's tweet alongside a picture of a man being stabbed in the neck. The picture seemed real and was exceptionally graphic. There was blood and the beginnings of a gaping wound. The brand entity icon account called Billy a dumb piece of shit in the quote tweet. Billy liked the threatening and violent tweet out of a vague hope that it would defuse things. He unpaused the video game and worriedly played for fifteen minutes.

He paused the game and checked Twitter and saw that the brand entity icon's quote-tweet had been deleted. The brand entity icon account had tweeted an apology about being hacked. The apology had several thousand likes. Billy received a direct message from the brand entity icon account. The brand entity icon account's direct message called him a *little bitch*. The brand entity icon account sent another direct message calling him a *fucking narc.* The brand entity icon account sent another direct message with a picture of the man being stabbed in the neck. It looked like the same man from the first photo being stabbed for a second time. Billy saw both neck wounds full of shiny blood. He saw that the brand entity icon account was typing another direct message.

He closed the Twitter application and put down his phone. He looked at the TV. He picked up his phone and opened the Twitter application. He saw that the brand entity icon account had sent another direct message. He looked at the message preview and thought, "This seems really bad," and laughed uncomfortably, waking his wife.

The Octopus

An octopus climbed out of the ocean. It wandered across the beach and onto the road. It got on a bus and went to the city center. It got on another bus and went to the airport. It went into the departures area and bought a ticket. It went through security and sat at the gate. It got on the airplane and flew to Washington, D.C. It took the shuttle to the National Mall. It waited in line for a tour of the White House. It broke off from the tour group and hid in an air vent. It spaced out for a while in the air vent. It left the air vent and went to the president's bedroom. It climbed into the president's bed. It pressed itself against the president's face. It waited for the president to stop breathing but then felt uncomfortable and confused and crawled off the president's face and moved onto the president's chest. It touched the president's face with its many tentacles. It felt the president breathing while thinking about the ocean. It moved off of the bed and sat on the windowsill. It felt tired and bored. It felt complex, inarticulable opinions about life and purpose, and crawled back into bed with the president. It felt unhappy and didn't know what would make it happy. It reasoned that possibly nothing could.

Putting Yourself Out There Just to Make Room for Yourself Version 2.0

❧

Jeff walked to his neighbor's house. He had a casserole. His neighbors had just had a baby. He understood that new parents needed casseroles, because of the baby. He wasn't entirely sure how it worked. He had to look up how to make a casserole. He had to buy a new casserole dish to make it in. He had to buy some ingredients he never bought before, like cooking spray and frozen potatoes. At the grocery store, someone was talking into a walkie-talkie about guns—something about making sure there were enough guns. Jeff had wondered then how many guns he could hold if he had to. He was still thinking about how many guns he could hold, max, when his neighbors answered the door. The guy was holding the baby and looked confused. The baby looked at Jeff. Jeff held up the casserole and said he had brought a casserole. The guy shifted his weight and looked down at the baby, then at the casserole, and then at Jeff. The guy wasn't wearing a shirt. He set the baby down on the floor and took the casserole into the house. Jeff looked at the baby and thought, "Baby." The guy came back and said thank you. Jeff asked how the mom was doing. The guy sighed while shaking his head. He looked down at the baby slowly fidgeting on the floor. He cleared his throat and said, "She's fine. You know, uh, she's good." Jeff looked at the guy's naked chest and arms and felt with some degree of confidence that they could both probably hold four or five guns if someone was really counting on them.

Doors

❧

Susan bought a gun that shot doors into things. The doors were small and led to incredible places.

She could shoot a door into another door and then both doors would lead to somewhere different. Like, the front door of her house led out into the world outside her house, where there was a street, a mailbox, some grass, some rocks, some garbage, and some other houses and other mailboxes and other patches of grass and rocks and garbage.

But the door she shot into it opened up to Alaska, to the inside of an apartment complex's front office in Anchorage.

Susan climbed through the little door. It didn't look like she'd fit but she knew better than to trust her instincts about stuff like that. And she thought Anchorage seemed better than Rochester, so why not.

One time she shot the gun into a tree and it led to the other side of another tree. Once she shot it at a bird and a whole mess of organs much too big for the bird leaked out all over the tree branch. The door led to the inside of a moose or something.

"How much for an apartment?" she asked the guy at the front desk.

"Seven hundred a month. Includes all utilities 'cept for internet."

"I'll take it," she said. "Lemme run to an ATM."

She walked around to the back of the building. Wind was blowing, cold and wet. She shot a whole bunch of doors into the ground—*bang! bang! bang!* —until she found one that opened up to a wad of cash tucked in someone's bottom drawer. The apartment was a one bedroom with a window that looked out over the bus stop. There were always the same people there, waiting for the bus. Going to work, going downtown, going to visit their families. Not everyone has a magic gun. Susan, did, though, which made her special.

She often thought about how she wasn't *actually* special because anyone could have bought the gun and be just as special as she was. No one thinks the drunk who bought a winning scratch-off ticket is any smarter or more handsome or nicer than anyone else. They just call him a lucky son of a bitch and daydream about how their own scratch-off tickets might make them special one day.

Susan didn't choose much about her life, but she did choose to buy the magical gun.

There wasn't much to do in Anchorage except drink and try to warm up and watch TV in her new apartment. Booze was cheap and the air was salty but the rest of it looked a lot like Rochester. Same shitty kinds of bars, same shitty coffee. Just more pictures of crabs everywhere and more beautiful, glorious mountains on the horizon. The mountains in upstate New York are more like dirty little mudpiles compared to the mountains in Alaska, she thought.

Pick any point on Earth and odds are that it's not your kind of place. Maybe no one speaks the language, maybe the food sucks, maybe there's nothing but a bunch of giant snakes and diseased swamp water for miles around. Most of the Earth is covered in ocean, infinite and terrifying. Some of the land is as dry as a bone. And some of the land is radioactive from old nuclear bomb tests. Other places are just full of dead bodies—cemeteries, burial grounds, mass burial pits in a war-torn African border town.

She wondered whether there was someplace where dead people might still go on living. Like an alternate dimension or a different planet or a special room in a church somewhere where God decided to do a miracle every once in a while for his favorite disciples.

She wondered whether she could shoot herself in the head, open the little door it'd make, and pull out a new brain, a happier, healthier, smarter, kinder, better brain and take it to the doctor and ask to get it implanted, or else climb through one of those hundreds of doors that look out over the ocean, dark and deep, just sink to the bottom and never come back up.

Forever Indebted to Yourself

~

For a long time, Billy fell asleep, then woke up; he couldn't stop. Every day he just did it, whatever it was, no matter what, then went to bed, and did it again. For example, once, he had to climb up the side of a building. People told him he had to, and if he didn't, they'd be mad, so he did it, and they told him via text message that they were impressed. Standing on top of the building, he had vaguely felt sure that being impressed was basically the same as being mad. He had regretted climbing the building, then, and decided not to respond. But he couldn't find the door to get back into the building, so he had to text someone for help.

The Very Good Dog

The very good dog slept in a little dog bed outside the toddler's room all night. In the morning, the dad woke up and peed. The very good dog woke up and trotted to the back door. The dad opened the back door and the very good dog trotted down the steps and into the grass and peed. The very good dog sat on the bottom stair and looked up at the phone lines that hung over the little back yard. The very good dog saw a squirrel scamper across the phone lines. The very good dog barked and ran after the squirrel. The squirrel got distracted by the barking maybe and fell from the phone line. The very good dog ran after the squirrel and cornered it against a concrete wall. The squirrel attempted to scamper up the concrete wall. The very good dog bit the squirrel in the neck. The very good dog shook its head around and snapped the squirrel's neck. The very good dog rolled around in the squirrel blood and ate a large amount of hot, raw squirrel meat and gnawed on the raw, hot squirrel bones. The dad opened the door and saw the dead squirrel remains and the blood-covered very good dog and said, "Holy shit." He shut the door. He thought vaguely about plastic bags, hoses, towels, calling the veterinarian, etc. He thought about love and joy in spite of the never-ending bullshit. He opened the door again and looked at the very good dog covered in blood and said, "Holy fucking shit" very quietly.

Public Transportation

Emo Phillips stands on a train. He thinks about all the fucked up people he knows and wonders if people think he's as fucked up as he thinks other people are. The train conductor/engineer/driver person clicks on the intercom and thanks everyone for riding the train. Emo Phillips feels like he has never been thanked for riding public transportation.

"Hey, am I fucked up?" Emo Phillips asks.

"What," says Dan Brown. Dan Brown is looking at an advertisement for furniture. The train conductor/engineer/driver person clicks on the intercom and apologizes for the slow pace of the train. Emo Phillips takes off his mittens. The advertisements for furniture are very sexually explicit—in one advertisement, there is a picture of two men having passionate sex on top of a dresser— and Dan Brown feels incredibly unloved. He doesn't want to be on the train anymore.

"Like, am I weird, I guess," Emo Phillips says. "Like, is there stuff weird about me. To people."

"Yeah, dude, uh...I guess. Or not," says Don Brown (easier to type than Dan Brown). The furniture advertisement seems really fucked up. "But yeah, probably." He imagines himself making love on top of a dresser for a photoshoot. He imagines himself being paid $7,000 in twenty-dollar bills for the photoshoot. He imagines not telling his lover about the photoshoot. He imagines using some of the money to buy a new dresser because of how good it was to be fucked on that kind of dresser as part of a photoshoot.

The train conductor/engineer/driver person clicks on the intercom and suggests that more people should get off at the next stop so the train can go faster, because of the weight of the people. Almost everyone on the train checks to see what the next stop is.

"What?" asks Emo Philips (one *l*, spell check seems cool with this). He is looking at the advertisement. The man penetrating the other man in the advertisement has an Emo Philips tattoo on his right shoulder. Emo Philips feels worried. He remembers that there is a furniture store at the next stop.

don brown (no caps) clarifies that he doesn't know what Emo is asking. They are lovers, and they are on the train, and The train conductor/engineer/driver person clicks on the intercom (copy pasting this now) and begins to cry into the microphone thing, pleading

Everything Is

Normal Life

The Literary Agent

I listened to a podcast about literary agents. The guy
on the podcast had cancer, he was dying—every day
he was dying a little bit more—and he was reflecting
on being a literary agent. He said that he had made
over ten million dollars as a literary agent. He said
that he used the money to buy the best, newest, most
experimental cancer treatment on the market. He
said the treatment had prolonged his life by about
two years, but now the cancer was really bad, worse
than before. He said he'd often wake up in a cold
sweat, having dreamt of seeing the cancerous tumors
breaking through his skin. He would dream about
the cancer ripping itself out of him, and in the dreams
he would touch the cancer and the cancer would be
warm and dark and pliable. He talked extensively
about these cancer dreams, how none of the doctors
could give him anything to quiet the dreams. He
dreamt about the cancer every night, and often the
dreams would feel like they lasted hours, days, or
weeks. He would sleep for five hours but dream for
twenty. He would sleep for ten hours but dream for
fifty. He would dream for days on end about the
cancer ripping itself out of his body, and during the
day he would obsess over these dreams, and the
cancer itself, the dreams of the cancer compounding
his real mortal fears of the cancer. Every day he

didn't die was another three or four days he had to live in fear and agony in his dreams. He spent more of his money on therapy, on hypnosis, on experimental new medications that would quiet his dreams, or that would let him lucidly dream, or would let him dream in fixed ways. He paid a hundred thousand dollars for a machine that cast special lights about his room and played bleating electronic pulses through tiny, wireless earbuds, all so he could sleep soundly, so he could sleep dreamlessly, but the machine was a failure, none of it worked. Each night the cancer was there, bursting out of his arms and legs and stomach, and he would often have to grab ahold of it and carry it, leaking blood and puss, along barren roads and sidewalks to an impossibly distant hospital. He spent so much money on the cancer treatment and the treatments for his dreams that he had to sell his houses, his boats, his cars, his precious works of art. His children began to plead with him so that they could be left some money after his immediate, unavoidable death. But he held out, he spent as much as he could, and he borrowed money, vast sums from his previous clients, from the millionaires whose manuscripts he had pitched and sold over his lifetime, and he'd lie to them, make them promises, tell them he was writing them into his will, that they would get the houses and boats and cars he had already pawned off. He destroyed every relationship he had ever had. He destroyed everything, and the last days of his life were being spent in complete isolation—he was unbearably alone, penniless, and depressed, and this podcast episode was most likely the last time he would ever speak to another person before the cancer finally destroyed him. He said the word *destroy*. That is how he described his own death: as the cancer *destroying* him, as his death as a type of *destruction*. He said he imagined himself as a statue of glass, and the cancer was a toddler tearing through the room. That's what he said: *a statue of glass*. Brad Listi repeated that back to him: *a statue of glass*. He couldn't think of anything else to say.

Splash Zone

It's a weird TV show where famous people have to do crimes. It's always trending online. Thom Yorke with a chainsaw was the season finale and he got ten people. They had cameras in the *splash zone*. There was a quick cut to the announcer and she did that smarmy told you so thing and said, "Yeah tha's righ' we callin' it a SPLASH zone." Thom Yorke is worth something like fifty million dollars. My dad texted me to ask if I knew who Thom Yorke was and I told him I had no idea. I don't know why I told him that I didn't know who Thom Yorke was. I kept thinking about all the blood in the splash zone and the cake at the end that Thom Yorke cut into with the chainsaw. My dad texted me to ask if I saw Thom Yorke cut into the cake with the chainsaw. He said, "He ruined the cake!" and I texted back, "lol." I couldn't tell if my dad was trying to connect with me with a joke or if he was seriously worried about the cake and not knowing which of the two possibilities was true made me realize that our relationship had been irreparably damaged. I looked it up. Thom Yorke is worth almost exactly fifty million dollars.

Coach

"Sport is one of the few things left that bind us with death," says Coach Timothy Burns, Riverton High School's newest football coach, over a slice of strawberry rhubarb pie over at Glennson's on Highway 41.

Tall, kind, and a star athlete himself, Coach Burns is a welcome addition to Riverton High's rich history of sporting excellence. Come along as I catch up with Coach Burns during a whirlwind tour of our little town, where we talk about football, the Riverton community, and some of the great things we can look forward to this fall.

"Sport is bound up in death," he continues, "bound up in its swift renunciation of the material world. When we pursue sport, we pursue death."

Joining the Riverton community after an impressive run of leading other high school football teams to state championships in both Kentucky and Indiana, I ask Coach Burns what drew him to Riverton High School. Is it our longtime standard of both academic and athletic excellence? Is it our impressive showings at every state conference? Is it the delicious local pies?

"I am here for no reason other than to subsist, like a roach who finds itself behind the stove in a condemned building. One needs money to even have the barest scrap of hope to suffer through life, so I pursue the scant opportunities that allow me to live. But I do not consider this life. We are surrounded by politicians and capitalists, the greatest threats to our crumbling society, and they shape what our lives may be. They insist we live surrounded by beggars, by thieves. Thieves of passion, thieves of thought itself. I extract what pittance I can from this great estate and squander it on baubles, on fetid meats and cheeses, on stale bread and spoilt wine, and this is what we call life. I run the boys in circles in exchange for a pittance. A pittance. The pay is an unconscionable insult, a true pittance, but, of course, all pay is an insult. And the rich are still like us, suicidal, but driven to insanity by their own wealth instead of poverty."

Coach Burns considers trying another slice of pie, eventually settling on a slice of good old-fashioned cherry. I ask if he's bulking up for the season, but he shakes his head no. "I do not run on the pitch. I refuse to toss a ball. I do not participate in the sport that I am condemned to coach, because sport offers us only great wounds. It always bears the threat of a wound deep enough to maim or kill. It offers us only pain," he adds.

Back downtown, looking out over our historic town square, we discuss how Riverton is a proud, family-focused community. Many of our star Riverton High athletes play on the same fields that their parents played on, so I ask Coach Burns about his own family. Where did he get the coaching bug? Did Mr. Burns spend his youth on the gridiron?

"My father believed in sport," Coach Burns tells me. "He did not play games, but rather *believed* in sport, believed in the *spirit of the game,* as he often put it. He was a brutal man, a horrible, tragic man, and he suffered immensely, terrorized by his own insanity. In his madness, he taught me to hunt. He taught me to embrace the hunt. My father taught me that the hunt is the last remaining sport, the last true sport, for it wholly embraces death, as he put it."

On the topic of hunting, I ask Coach Burns if he plans on taking advantage of the wonderful hunting grounds just west of Route 82—and I want to remind him, and all of our readers, that county hunting licenses are only available for another two weeks!

"Hunting for deer is an aberration. To hunt for deer is to embrace insanity, to embrace madness. It is a pitiful, futile endeavor. To hunt is to cower, to hide and ambush. It is thus shameful, and no man alive truly knows his own shame. We are condemned to be numb to our own shame, for it is the only way that we may live. The hunt is especially shameful, a truly disgusting depravity, but it is also empowering, and this power gives the hunt its appeal, but also its sadness. It is a pure sadness, it is futility, and the meat of the deer is poisoned, it is vile—venison is a putrid meat, and it begins stinking as soon as it is sloughed off the bone. It stinks in the pot, it stinks in the stew, it putrifies the air in the entirety of the kitchen. Its smell haunts the cupboards, like a stain. And nothing can be done to rid the house of its stench, you must destroy the house, abandon any hope of living a *normal* life in such a house. Venison stinks when you chew it, it stinks in your gullet. The putrid meat expands in your bowels, it constricts the intestines, it constricts the appetite—it murders you slowly, clogging your organs with its horrifying stink. It constricts the spirit, nothing but a foul and rotten meat that constricts the soul. But, of course, there is no soul, there can be nothing holy in us—there cannot be anything of heaven in us, because we are depraved, because we are no better than the foul venison. We are the meat that rots, the rotten meat on the bone, and we stink from birth until death, from when no soul is wrought to when no soul escapes. But the venison meat constricts the soul all the same, there is no question of this. No, no, for this reason, hunting a deer is pure madness. The hunt is a purely *mad* thing, but even then, it is a performance, as my father said, a *debased dance,* as he put it to me once. But it is an off-kilter dance, purely deranged, more of a *fumbling* than anything respectable or sane. It is not a *bilateral embrace,* as he often called it, I argue—the hunter is never in danger, we are never truly in danger while on the hunt, although we pretend we are, we pretend that the hunt may destroy us at any minute. We are *cowards* in the hunt, hiding behind artifice, behind steel, lead, gunpowder, and we are never truly threatened, we are never truly confronted with our own mortality during the hunt. The hunt is a farce, a brutal, murderous farce, it is a morbid ridiculousness, and nothing redeems the hunter. My father knew this, and he grappled often with its ridiculousness—it is what ultimately killed him, the sad disingenuity of his life's passion driving him to suicide, killed by his own rifle. Hunting a deer is horrifying, and eating its meat is even more so. No, I do not hunt."

Next, I bring Coach Burns to Dan's Sporting Goods and Trophy Pavilion, where we get a sneak peek at the newest line of jerseys and helmets for this year's football season.

I ask Coach Burns what he thinks of the new, breathable, ergonomic designs.

"The mask is not to protect the face," he says, showing off a brand-new Riverton Hawk football helmet provided by a generous donation from the owner of Dan's Sporting Goods and Trophy Pavilion himself, Dan Rutherford. "The mask exists simply to prevent the player from his more primal inclinations, from gnashing out—it is to *enclose* the player and protect us from the gnashing, from the overbearing desire to lash out. The mask is for the bite, to *contain* the bite, to prevent the gnashing from drawing blood, from giving the player a taste of *his true goal*. For sport to have any meaning, it must be played upon the precipice of pain, surrounded by a sea of blood, and it must make the player desire to bathe in this blood, to splash about in the pain of others. The players, the children of this town—for that is what they are, men, yes, but still children, horrible children, enraged children consumed by death and the desire to kill *and* to die, which is important, they do not only wish to *kill* for sport but also to *be killed* for sport—they feel the draw of the bite. They are mad, they are utterly insane, mad from birth and socialized into an even worse madness, one that leads directly to death. Their brains are corrupted by violence, and this corruption is the human spirit itself—it is the only outcome, our own spirits corrupt us and cause us to worship pain and embrace death. They are natural horrors, the children, and I fear them, and I often cannot sleep for this fear. I suffer a great insomnia fueled by an unbearable anxiety, I toss and writhe in my cot, waking from nightmares of the children and their insane desires for carnage, gnashing at me on the pitch, clawing at me in the locker room, plotting against me while perched like crows upon the bleachers. I often writhe in my cot and I grasp at my face to feel the mask, to feel for the helmet. The helmet—and the mask, together with it—is a *cage*. I dream of this cage often. Almost nightly I dream of this cage and how it encloses around my brain. The cage does not protect me, in fact it *contains* me, and thus it terrorizes me, and I often cannot sleep until two, three in the morning. And when I wake at five, I am not well. I do not rest well when I dream of the cage, and I often do dream of the cage."

"Agree"

So I'm trying to vote. Because it's an election. And there's these computer...things...for voting. I have to touch a screen and it does the vote stuff. So there's a screen with instructions. I read the instructions without really paying attention. Okay. Next page. More stuff. No voting yet. This sucks. I'm worried about how long this will take. I touch a button on the screen that says, "Agree." It's doing that little circle thing. Okay. I'm waiting for something. Okay. There's some stuff about voting. This seems good. I touch a button on the screen that says, "Agree." It's doing that little circle thing. Okay. There's a ballot measure. I touch the screen to see my options. There are more options than I thought there would be. I scroll down. I touch a button on the screen that says, "No." It's doing that little circle thing. The screen reloads. It's mostly the same but the buttons moved a little bit. And there's the president's face. Alright. It says he's running for congress. Shit. I look to see if anyone else is having problems. The people seem like they're doing okay. There's a sign taped on my voting machine that says, "No Talking." I look around some more. I think I need a poll worker or someone. But there's also a sign that says, "No Looking Around," too. Alright. The screen changes and now it says that the president is running for vice president. I want to look at my phone to check the time but that seems not allowed maybe. Someone by the door is talking quietly about pancakes. The screen has a timer on it. I vote third party so I can move on. I don't really care about the vice president. I'm not sure what the vice president does. It's back on the instructions screen. I touch a button on the screen that says, "Agree." It's doing that little circle thing. Maybe I can start over. Okay, no, there's a new screen, just a bunch of pictures of fat men. Wait. Okay, no. I touch a button that says, "Forward." It goes back to the instructions. The timer seems stuck. I really want to look around but I'm worried about the signs. I feel warm. I think I can smell pancakes. The screen is blank now. So I can see things reflected in it. And I see the president walk in. And I see people looking around and taking pictures. The screen turns back on. Shit, that's a lot of buttons. Oh no. I'm looking for the right button but I keep pushing the wrong one because the screen is kind of rotating. And it goes blank again. Goddammit. The president walks up behind me. I can see his reflection in the blank screen. This seems really bad. I start to turn around but he says, "No." He touches my shoulder. The screen turns back on and it lists some of my personal information and asks me to confirm. I close my eyes. I breathe. I can smell the president (we wear the same cologne) and I can hear him running his tongue across his front teeth maybe. I open my eyes. There's only one button on the screen and it says, "Helicopter." There's a little picture of a helicopter, too. It's cute. The president starts rubbing my back and I don't really feel like getting into the rest of what happens right now—it's a long story.

Imaginative Play

I sent an email to the farm people to see if they had any openings on Tuesdays for the farm babies thing. You, like, let your kid play on the farm. The website thing mentions dirt a lot and says it costs $8 for like an hour, which is pretty good, compared to other stuff, like the indoor play places with a bunch of toys or whatever, which cost $15. This one also probably involves animals, or, like, animals would be present, within view of the farm babies activity stuff. Animal-adjacent farm babies. You could see some chickens probably while playing in the dirt. Which sounds pretty nice to me. I'd like that, at least. I was reading about farms and shit, like, all this good stuff about them. Like in the dirt or whatever, there's all these different kinds of bacteria you don't get exposed to at parks or whatever. And the plants are good for you...the sunlight. I don't know, there's just all this stuff about it. Good for babies because of the stimulation, different kinds of stimulation, like the colors and movement or whatever. It's like back-to-nature kinda stuff but different, I guess, because the animals and the kinds of plants, like, symbiotic...like agriculture...stuff...old school human shit, uh, grains and fungus or whatever. And $8 is a fucking steal, too. Where else do you get to see goats and stuff that's not a petting zoo? Cows...you can see cows probably.

Man, imagine our baby touching a cow...haha no but, I mean, you probably can't touch the cows but like, imagine. I haven't heard back from the farm people though so it's probably a no-go. No farm babies, no chickens. I'm all excited for it but it's not gonna happen. Like, I'm all pumped up but it's probably not gonna happen. No cows, I guess. Fuck. Wait hold on I just got an email. Oh shit, N I C E

We Looked Under Your Skin and Only Found More Skin!

I bought a cold brew coffee and went to the doctor's office! I drank all the coffee in the waiting room! There was footage of a bombing on the TV in the waiting room! Twenty-three Americans were dead! Several hundred non-Americans were dead! The bombing on the TV took place at a doctor's office in another country! The waiting room smelled like lavender! The cold brew tasted like chocolate!

A nurse made me stand on a scale! I was over two hundred pounds! The nurse measured my height! I was six feet exactly! He told me to go into a small room and get naked and put on a paper dress! I got naked in the small room! I put on the paper dress! The nurse knocked on the door! I told him to come in! He came in and asked me questions about my mental health! I said that I felt like the world would be better off without me between zero and two times per month! I said that I drank fewer than five alcoholic drinks per month! I said that I felt like my daily life was impossible to get through between zero and two times per month! The nurse typed my answers into a computer and left!

I read a poster about diabetes! I felt worried that the doctor would discover I had diabetes! Or some other disease! And that I would live a life of pain and daily medication! Or die young! I wanted to blow up in a bombing in some other country! Or maybe not! Maybe I just wanted to drink more coffee!

The doctor came in! She asked about my mental health! She asked about my diet! She asked about my job! She asked about what method of birth control I use with my wife! I tried to respond but I didn't know the proper term for "pulling out"! So I hesitated! I thought of the term "coitus interruptus" but felt that maybe that was some kind of joke term you're not supposed to use with doctors! So I hesitated some more! The doctor asked me if I had withdrawn! I didn't know what she meant! I thought maybe she was asking if I had emotionally withdrawn from intimacy with my wife due to mental health reasons! I felt primed by all the questions about mental health so that sounded like a reasonable interpretation of her question! So I repeated the word "withdrawn" in a questioning tone! The doctor looked visibly frustrated! I was getting an erection from thinking about sex with my wife! My erection was touching the inside of the paper dress! I was worried that the doctor would want to touch my testicles to check for cancer while I had an erection! The doctor began an elaborate hand maneuver where she pulled her hand through a half-circle formed by her other hand! The hand motion made me think of a wilting flower! The doctor asked me if I withdrew my penis from my wife's vagina prior to ejaculation during intercourse! I said that I did! The doctor entered information about how I withdrew my penis from my wife's vagina prior to ejaculation during intercourse into the computer! After some other questions my erection went away! I felt fat and terrible-looking under my paper dress! The doctor didn't touch my testicles!

The doctor said that I seemed fine! Then she left the room! I put on my clothes! There was a hole in my sock! I went to the lab and had blood drawn! There was a poster about how to not be stressed out! It said I should take a nap! It said I should ride my bike! It said I should watch a movie! It said I should go for a walk! It said I should light a candle! It said I should meditate! It said I should pet a dog! It said I should eat some cake! It said I should listen to music! It said I should take a bath! It said I should call a friend! It said I should practice deep breathing! It said I should count the stars! It said I should watch the clouds! It said I should go to a museum! It said I should draw a picture! It said I should read a book of poetry! It said I should do some gardening! It said I should sing a song! It said I should make love! It said I should write a joke! It said I should go dancing! It said I should buy some flowers! It said I should drink some tea! It said I should write a letter to a friend! It said I should watch the rain! It said I should clean my pantry! It said I should do stretches! It said I should eat some ice cream! It said I should write a story!

I went home and looked at the internet! I got an e-mail from the doctor's office! I didn't have diabetes! I didn't have clinical depression! I was totally fine! That night I withdrew my penis from my wife's vagina prior to ejaculation during intercourse! EVERYTHING WAS TOTALLY FINE!

I'd keep going on it. There's something to this.

I put trash bags up on the walls for decoration. It looks good, like there are trash bags on the walls, which is good, to me. It feels festive. I wanted it to feel different and festive, like, festive in a different way, being in the room, and the trash bags on the walls is making that happen. Some people came in and walked around slowly. I watched them look around and walk and talk and eat snacks and stuff. Some of them touched the trash bags while speaking quietly. I enjoyed the sound of the rustling of the trash bags over them speaking quietly or just walking around. I haven't really attached the trash bags that securely so they're rustling, like, a lot. They're pretty loose. I used, like, maybe two pieces of tape per trash bag, for a few of the trash bags, for example. Some of the people talked quietly in one of the corners near the bar and I assume they were talking about how good the trash bags look. It felt good to see them talking about how the trash bags look. This is just a normal kind of party, you know, but just a little bit different, because of the trash bags. I asked my friend Suzanne what she thought of the trash bags and she smiled and said they looked pretty good. Suzanne is really solid. You'll like her, I think. Here, come over here, I'll introduce you.

Savoring the Single Mulberry that Cracked the Earth in Half

I spilled all the yogurt on the floor. I'm putting yogurt back into the container. Into the tub thing. It's a big tub. It's a lot of yogurt. Two spoons to be quicker. Not actually that quick. Trying one spoon plus a hand to, like, wall the yogurt in. Biiig scoops. Typed three i's on accident but it seems good, like a branding thing. Biiiiig scoops. Okay, the spoon still sucks. Just my hands, just using my hands. Fuck it. Yogurt everywhere, no time. They're just hands. Yogurt isn't bad for your hands. It's probably good for your hands. And the yogurt is more important. It's like thirty dollars' worth of yogurt, that thin whole milk yogurt. If this were Greek yogurt it'd be easy. Greek yogurt's thick as shit. You could just pick it up like a baseball. But this is the runny yogurt. It just keeps spreading out. It's lumpy but not that lumpy. I always wonder about the lumps. Should yogurt be lumpy? It's probably fine. Goddamn it all. Not gonna lick my fingers. Not yet. This is probably ruining all the yogurt. But I gotta try. I have to try and save the yogurt. You can't get that $30 back. If you can save $20, that's good. $10 is worth it. Even saving $2.50 worth of this yogurt is worth it. Scoop, slop, scoop, slop. Make it a Viking song. Heave, ho, motherfucker. Yogurt up, yogurt down. This doesn't look right. Lots of spots and specks. Off-white yogurt. Probably no good. I can't remember the last time I washed my hands. Living alone means I don't have anyone to give a yeast infection to. That used to be my problem in high school—I gave Marla yeast infections like every two weeks because I never washed my hands. She used yogurt to fix them, somehow. What the fuck was that. Yogurt fixing yeast infections. Yogurt as vagina medicine. $30 dollars' worth. I started washing my hands so I could finger her more. Then we broke up and I stopped. I never did get back into the habit. It saves money. Saves on soap. Live frugally. Less is more. Save the whales. Save the yogurt. Heave, ho, heave, ho. This isn't that much yogurt. I should give up. No, it's a lot. It's worth it. But I gotta take a break. It's not spreading out as much anymore. It's stabilized. I can stop for a second. I'm sweating. It's so hot. Not used to hunching over like this. Feeling kinda dizzy. Stood up too fast. Need to eat more yogurt. Maybe I'm low in iron. I'm breathing. I should wash my hands. I should go to the doctor. Push-ups, dead lifts. That's how it goes. Bigger, better, faster, stronger. Small steps. Eat yogurt, that was a step. Gut bacteria, protein, healthy fats. And it's cheap. $30 goes a long way. It felt like a good start. Gotta look out for myself. I'm all on my own. If I don't scoop it all up, what else am I going to do? I'm not going to, like, hose off the floor. I don't own any hoses. I don't own any mops. I have to do this no matter what. So I might as well do it now. I have yogurt on my hands already. God, there's yogurt everywhere. And there's sweat everywhere. Can't scratch my balls. Don't do it. More steps: buy more underwear, then wear the underwear. Gotta get a list together. Marla had lots of lists. My hands are sweaty. Jesus. Okay. Salty yogurt is a thing. It's okay. It's a European thing. I should google it to be sure. Put it on the list. The yogurt in the tub looks kind of...bad. It looks sandy. There's sand on the floor. Dunno why. But I've never cleaned my floor. I don't own any brooms. I don't own many...anythings...or something. I should buy a broom. Here's the list: $30 yogurt. $30 soap. $30 underwear. $30 broom. Use the fuck out of it all. Biiiig sweeps, baby, biiig sweeps, girl. I could pitch a jingle. Piiitch a jiiingle. Okay. Hooo-boy. I can do this. Think about the future. Think about tomorrow. Think about eating yogurt and living a good life. Scoop, slop, scoop, slop. Feels like a metaphor. I should call Marla. No, she's dead. Okay. I think I saved, like, $15 worth of yogurt. That's pretty good.

Normal Life 1

I wake up and I feel like the world will someday be a good place. I brush my teeth and I think the best years of my life are ahead of me. I drink coffee in the park and I imagine being a mother, bringing new life into the world, raising a good person who will bring joy to others and contribute to society in a positive way. I go to work and I think about the good things my company is doing and all the challenges I will face and grow from. I eat lunch and I think about my body using the food for energy and strength. I leave work and I think about the trains bringing new opportunities to people across the city. I pay my bills and I think about how I am helping create wealth and opportunity and purpose for all of the billions of people on the planet. I eat dinner and I think about all the good dinners I will eat throughout my life. I watch Netflix and I imagine doing so with a caring and loving partner who will stroke my hair and kiss me on the temple and hold me when I sleep. I go to bed and I think about resting my body for the next day. I think about tomorrow and I feel optimistic. I think about the rest of my life and feel good.

Normal Life 2

Girl scouts sell their cookies at the train station. Every day they yell to the people boarding and exiting the trains that they are selling cookies and that you can use a credit card to buy the cookies. Some of the girl scouts accosted a woman who was trying to ignore them. They surrounded her and brandished the boxes of cookies at her and told her that she should buy cookies. She told the girl scouts to fuck off and tried to push her way through them, but she had a hard time because she was, at the same time, trying to not touch them. The girl scouts followed her through the turnstile in a compact line so that the turnstile buzzed loudly to indicate that someone was attempting to access the train area without paying. The woman stood by the edge of the tracks while the girl scouts yelled at her and called her a fucking bitch and told her to buy cookies. When the train was coming, one of the girl scouts pushed her onto the tracks. All the girl scouts waited for the girl scout who pushed the woman to say a badass line like in a movie or something but she couldn't think of anything cool to say on the spot and looked visibly frustrated and embarrassed, and then the train conductor stopped the train early so he wouldn't run over the woman. Then the woman climbed out from the train track area and pointed at the girl scout who pushed her and told her to go fuck herself. The girl scout's mom swiped her card to access the platform and ran up with a box of cookies and told her to have a free box and that she was sorry. The woman took the box of cookies and boarded the train and went to work. The woman ate all the cookies in one sitting. The woman is me. I am the woman. They were thin mints.

Normal Life 3

There's a shark that lives behind me. Whenever I leave my apartment, he's behind me. When I drink my coffee, he's behind me. When I go to work, he's behind me. He scrunches himself up when I'm sitting on the toilet. He hangs out in the back seat when I'm stuck in traffic. He sits on the chair by the window when I eat takeout and watch TV on the couch. He's behind me when I brush my teeth. He's behind me when I stop by the liquor cabinet before bed. He's behind me when I go to sleep. He's behind me when I wake up from a bad dream. He's behind me when I look out the window in the middle of the night. He's behind me when I breathe onto the glass and fog it up. He's behind me when I trace a heart around his foggy reflection.

Normal Life 4

Just before midnight, I started taking a shower. I left the lights off. The word "hidden" was stuck in my head. It was hot and dark in the shower. I was hidden from things. I didn't know what things. I felt like I wasn't sure "what things were," or something, like as part of it. The shower was keeping me a secret from stuff. *Hush, hush.* That's what the water was saying. It was nice. I used organic shampoo and charcoal soap. I imagined the hot water never ending. I imagined living forever in the hot dark shower. Someone came looking for me but they couldn't find me. I was just standing in the shower, in the dark. I thought: *Hidden. Successful.* They left. I decided that I wouldn't go to work in the morning. That's the first decision I've made that will have a positive outcome in my life. I couldn't turn off the shower. I stumbled around in the dark. It sounded like I was someone else but it was just me. The shower stall was huge, and I wandered for a few days. The water never ended and I kept thinking about how I forgot to do shit, but it was okay, it was whatever. The cat came in and looked at me. It exploded and I saw its blood and organs and stuff. No, that didn't happen. I told the cat to explode. *Explode yourself,* I thought, telekinetically. No, wait, telephrastically. I thought about what the word is, what's that word? I thought, *Antipathy.* I was trying to think if it was *antipathically* instead. No, it's not. The cat looked at me. I didn't want the cat to die. I still don't want the cat to die. I asked the cat not to die, *telephatically*. No, that's not right, either. Shit. I turned off the water and toweled off and got dressed and fed the cat and considered wandering off into the desert. Might be good, maybe.

Normal Life 5

I played in the woods with my toddler. I carried my toddler out of the woods to the parking lot. I buckled my toddler into the car seat. I closed the door. A man stood by the next car over in the lot. He asked me if it was colder in the woods. I didn't know how to respond. I looked at the woods. The trees were very spread out. It seemed impossible for the temperature to be any different inside the woods than in the parking lot next to the woods. I looked at the man. I said the temperature was good. I said that the trees were kind of sparse. The man nodded like he understood. He started taking off his shirt. I got in the car and backed out onto the road. I looked at the man through the passenger window. He started taking off his pants. I put the car into drive. I saw the man crouch and pull down his underwear—I saw his penis bounce as he stood up. I drove down the road, changing radio stations while my toddler played with a toy goose. I put in a CD and rolled down the window. I took off my hat and gloves. I thought about how the woods probably were kind of cold. I thought about the man's penis—how it bounced, how it shone in the sun, etc.

Normal Life 6

Free form jazz in your ass. I'm serious. It's cheap—twenty bucks. Crisp bills only, though. You go down one of those dank little city stoops, like, the ones always full of leaves and trash. You knock on the door. You gotta show ID. Doesn't matter who you are. Jazz in the ass is 21+. They've got a full bar, some pinball machines. They opened up after the smoking ban so it's pretty nice inside. Doesn't feel like a shit dungeon. In the back, that's where you find the jazz. They've got dudes on trumpets, sax, you name it. Three-piece throwback guys, too. Some of that *sweepa sweepa sweepa bomb bom bom* shit. I've never done it but I know a buncha people who dig it. They say shit like that there, like, "Dig it, man." It's dumb but whatever, they say it's good. They do it *twenty for twenty*: throw your crisper in the bowl and you get twenty minutes of that good jazz right up your ass. I don't know—could be your kinda thing.

Normal Life 7

We went out to the new frozen yogurt place. The floor and walls were covered in blue and white tiles. It smelled like chlorine. There were no employees. The tiles made everything echoey and loud. We tried to stay quiet but it was hard. There was a sink on the wall. There was a toilet against the wall. The yogurt was delicious. No one else came in. We didn't know how to pay for the yogurt. I ate some more yogurt. My husband got up to look for the bathroom. He couldn't find the bathroom. I went up to the yogurt station. There were six different flavors of yogurt. There were twenty-six different toppings for the yogurt. I tried to remember where we had parked but couldn't really visualize the parking lot. My husband looked at the toilet in the middle of the room. He looked at me. I put maraschino cherries on my yogurt. My husband unbuckled his belt. I ate one of the cherries. It was delicious.

Normal Life 8

I held my breath. I watched the stopwatch. I waited five minutes. I didn't have to breathe. I was fine. I continued not breathing. I went for a run but didn't breathe. I went shopping but didn't breathe. I took a long bath and lay under the water for forty-five minutes. I did other stuff but without having to breathe. I lived the rest of my life doing normal life stuff but without having to breathe. I otherwise did no extraordinary things in my short life and my funeral was sparsely attended.

Like a Car That Looks Exactly Like a Slightly Smaller Car

I found a horse in my yard—well, not my yard, but, like, this space behind my apartment. The horse was gray. I had never seen a gray horse before. I tried to think about what I knew about horses. I knew there were white horses, black horses, and brown horses. The horse was eating flowers that the landlord had planted. I don't know why he planted flowers in the weird space behind my apartment. The horse wasn't eating the trash in the space behind my apartment. I might as well call it a yard, because that's kind of what it was, but it wasn't mine, because I didn't own it. I thought maybe the horse was the landlord's horse. I had a running list of things to look up—can horses be gray, do horses eat flowers, do horses eat trash, do landlords own horses, does my landlord own a horse, is it my yard if I'm just a tenant, can I plant flowers in the yard, can I ride horses that are in the yard (compare with: can I sit in the chair in the yard, which I had asked my landlord when I moved in, and the answer was yes, I could sit in the chair). The horse finished eating every flower in the yard. I felt uncomfortable thinking that I had "found" the horse. I was told to consider reevaluating my initial reactions to novel situations and experiences in therapy several months prior. I reevaluated by initial reaction. I thought that maybe the horse had "found" me. Maybe the horse had some purpose for me. Maybe the horse was waiting for me to do... something. Or maybe...anything. I couldn't think of things anymore. I felt tired. I went to sleep on the couch. I woke up. The landlord was in the yard, talking to the horse. The landlord pointed at me through the window while speaking sternly to the horse. The horse looked at me; I hid behind the couch. I worried about the horse. I worried about what the landlord was saying about me to the horse. I was monumentally depressed, and I would continue to be for many more years—this was only one terrible day out of thousands.

A Beautiful Hill

A woman came to me at the graveyard with her husband's corpse, to buy a grave, now that he was dead. I need a good plot of land, the woman said, he deserves a good spot, my husband. He needs a deep grave, she said, a good one, a deep one. Somewhere on the hill, she said, somewhere it can be good and deep. I nodded, took the keys off the wall and unlatched the iron gate and led her and her husband's corpse out into the yard. I motioned with my arm for them to survey the place, to look for somewhere fitting, a place for a grave well-suited for the husband's corpse among the other graves. Her husband's corpse kicked at a tuft of moss, sucked on his teeth. We have a few hills, I said, yes, we have a few hummocks, a few different places, a wide variety. Yes, she said, I see, you have some variety here, quite a large plot of land. Very large, I said, lots of variety here. Her husband's corpse looked to one of the hills in the back, our biggest hill, over in the back under the old oak trees. A good hill, there, he said, that hill, there, with the trees. Yes, with the trees, said the woman, a beautiful hill, that one. Our best hill, I said, and our best trees. Are those oak? she asked. Yes, I said, oaks, all of them oaks. Beautiful trees, she said, those oaks. Good shade on that hill, I said, good protection from the breeze, too. Her husband's corpse nodded, his eyes meandering with each nod. But I like a good breeze, he said, a breeze is nice, you know. Of course, I said, especially in the summer, a good breeze is a beautiful thing. Yes, he said, a good breeze can be a good thing. Cools you off, she said, a nice breeze in the summer months. Of course, I said, even with the trees, you can still catch a fine breeze on that hill. On such a fine hill, the woman said, of course, I would imagine so. Yes, I said, it's our very best hill, with our best oaks, the best breezes. Expensive, though, the woman said, I imagine it's expensive on that hill. Yes, I suppose you could say it's expensive, I said, relatively so, yes, it is our nicest bit of land, the hill with the oak trees and the breeze. But not too windy, said her husband's corpse, it shouldn't be too windy. No, not too windy, I said, no, of course, not too windy. But a breeze is nice, she said, a good breeze on a good hill is a very nice thing. Of course, I said, always a very nice breeze on that hill. We examined the hill from our spot, the breeze stirring the oak leaves. But not too much of a breeze, her husband's corpse said, not a strong wind, not a blustery hill, not too much wind. No, I said, of course not, only a fine breeze on that hill. Only ever a slight breeze? he asked, never too much wind? Exactly right, I said, breezy without being too windy. The best hill, said the woman, but also the most expensive. Of course it's expensive, said her husband's corpse, but that's of no concern, no concern for us at all.

We walked to the hill with the oaks and I leaned on my spade as they examined the ground. Do you rake? asked the woman, do you rake often around here, under the oaks? Twice a week, I said, I rake the whole grounds twice a week in the fall. Twice a week, said her husband's corpse, even up on this hill. Of course, I said, this is our best hill, it's our best bit of land, it deserves a good raking when the leaves fall. Do you use a metal rake? he asked. Of course, I said, only metal tools here. No plastic, said the woman, high quality tools only. Only the best tools, I said, only metal tools here. I tapped my metal spade on a stone, for emphasis. Only the best tools on our best hill, I said, which is full of the best graves. Full? asked the woman, full of graves? Not quite, I said, no, not so full. But not empty? asked her husband's corpse, not a desolate hill? Exactly, I said, neither empty nor full. And not too many rocks? asked her husband's corpse, here on the hill, not too many rocks, not many stray stones, when you use the metal rake? He motioned as if to rake, his rotted skin sloughing from the bones of his fingers. Not many stones, I said, just a few stones on this hill. I wouldn't want to hear so much scraping, twice a week, he said, not too much scraping but rather quiet, a good quiet. Of course, I said, few stones around, a good clean hill, and very quiet, even when raking. We stood, considering the hill.

So, there you have it, I said, this is the best hill we have, the best hill with the best view and the best trees. But also the most expensive, said the woman, more expensive than the other hills. I suppose so, I said, yes, the best hill does demand a fair price. But that is no concern, said her husband's corpse, no concern at all. What do you think? I asked, about this hill here? This should be fine, he said, a fine hill to be buried in. It is indeed the finest hill, I said. A very fine hill, said the woman, yes. But also the most expensive, I said, we do have other hills. Of course, said the woman, I'm sure they must all be very nice. But this one, said her husband, this is the nicest hill.

I sent them away and began to dig. I dug deep, a good deep grave in the very best hill. A wide, deep grave, deep enough to keep out the wind and the rain and the sound of the rake, even if there are few stones, because there are always stones, and so there is always the chance of a metallic scrape of the rake against a stone, especially toward the end of autumn, when it is quiet and the clouds are low, and the sound would carry in all directions. So I dug the grave deep and wide, a good grave on our nicest hill with the oaks and very few stones. The woman returned with her husband's corpse and examined the grave. We all peered in at its depth, of which I was exceptionally keen to show them.

A good depth, I said, deeper than most. Very deep, said the woman, I've never seen such a deep grave. Yes, very deep, I said, we don't dig them this deep, usually, but I dug this one especially deep. They don't dig them this deep, the woman said to her husband's corpse, but here, this one is very deep. All well and good, he said, it is deep, of course it's deep. But, I said. But, he said, how deep doesn't matter if the soil is light. If the soil is light? I asked, if the soil's too light? That's right, he said, the soil must be dense. Dense soil, I said, densely packed. Right, he said, the deepest grave is nothing with cheap soil. I see, I said, of course, the soil must be dense. How is the soil here? asked the woman, how dense is it? We have many kinds of soil, I said, many kinds to choose from, from all throughout the grounds here. But mostly thin soil, said her husband's corpse, cheap soils, all of them, I imagine. Some dense soils, I said, we have many kinds, but at different costs, as you can imagine. All different prices, said the woman, for the different soils. All local soils? asked her husband's corpse, all from this lot here? Mostly, I said, mostly local, but some others, too. Imported? asked the woman, you have imported soils? Yes, I said, some imported soils. Expensive, said the woman, those imported soils, I would imagine. Expensive, yes, but of higher densities, I said, different compositions, all especially good for a deep grave. Expensive, said the woman, the denser soils, more expensive. Before we decide on the grave, we must decide on the soil, said her husband's corpse, the soil is of utmost importance. Of course, I said, we have a few kinds I could show you, all different densities.

I led them to the soils and we examined them. The woman peered into the barrels with her hands in her pockets. These here are all local, her husband's corpse said, in these barrels. That's right, I said, from all over the grounds here, but also some others, from nearby, from farther north. Canadian soils? the woman asked, you mean soil imported from Canada? No, I said, not quite so far north as that. Canadian soil, said her husband's corpse, that would be too much of a bother. Perfectly good soil, though, I said, not Canadian, but close, nearly Canadian. Better than Canadian soil, he said, denser than Canadian soil. Of course, I said, nicer soil on this side of the border, all told. Lots of good kinds of soil from here as well, said the woman, gorgeous colors, these. These are the local ones, I said, very good soils, all sourced from these very grounds. And they're cheaper? asked the woman, cheaper than the northern soils? Cheaper, yes, I said, but still very good, still quite dense. And nothing from farther south? asked her husband's corpse, nothing from south of here? No, all local, I said, or from farther north, near Canada, as I said, but still very good. But nothing from south of here, said her husband's corpse. Right, I said, nothing like that here. Well, these look fine, said the woman, these local soils, they look dense to me, very good. But all local, said her husband's corpse, and these local soils are all sandy or loamy or rocky, nothing good and dense like from farther south. Did you have anything in mind? I asked, from anywhere in particular?

The woman looked back toward the hill with the oaks. Her husband's corpse limped toward her as bits of bone and old blood peered out from under his torn trousers. They spoke quietly and I leaned on my spade. It was a beautiful day. The woman dug around in her purse and withdrew her cell phone. She sighed.

We can take a rideshare, her husband's corpse said, that might be the quickest way. A rideshare? I asked, a rideshare to fetch soil for the grave? You know how much we need, he said, you can decide how much we need for such a deep and wide grave. Of course, I said, but it will be a fair amount for this grave. Yes, I'm sure, he said, a rather large amount of soil for such a fine grave. How far is it? I asked, how far are we going for the soil?

The woman looked down at her phone, then motioned toward the barrels of soil. The van is on its way, the woman said. I'll need to close early if we'll be gone long, I said, although it's a shame to close so early and lose out, on potential business. Yes, the woman said. Where are we going? I asked, if you don't mind me asking, where are we off to? Pittsburgh, said her husband's corpse. We're going to Pittsburgh? I asked, someone agreed to drive us all the way to Pittsburgh? Yes, said the woman, I suppose so. Of course, said her husband's corpse, yes, of course, that is their job, to drive, so they will drive us to Pittsburgh to get the best soil. Very good soil near Pittsburgh, they say, I said. Will it be okay for the hill? asked the woman, is it okay to use soil all the way from Pittsburgh? Of course, said her husband's corpse, it's fine, it's the best soil, the very best soil. But there will be a fee, I said, if I am to accompany you as far as Pittsburgh for the soil. A fee, said the woman, an additional fee. Of course, said her husband's corpse, as expected, this is work, valuable work, a fee is no matter, no matter at all, and so we will pay what we need to pay, we will compensate you as needed. It will have to be a generous fee, I said, for so much time, for so much travel, for so much work. Money is no matter, he said, no, it is the grave that matters. We are here for a good grave, I suppose, said the woman. The money is no matter at all, he said, only the grave matters, nothing else, we can spend as much as needed, as high as your fees can go, set them there, and we will pay them. But these local soils, said the woman, they all seem nice to me, the local ones, nice and local and dense, I would say, though I am no expert, surely we don't need to go through so much trouble. Absolutely not, said her husband's corpse, no, absolutely not, none of these local soils will do, just terrible, all of them, look at them, they are full of rocks, of twigs, of old bits of bone and dung, no, absolutely not. The trip will be so expensive, she said, and then the soil itself, we will have to pay for the soil, too, and we will have to pay to transport it back, and we will have to pay for the truck, for the soil and the truck together. No, it's my grave, he said, it's my grave and none of these soils will do, no, we will fetch some better soil, all of us. I refuse, he said, I simply refuse to be entombed in such terrible soil, to be surrounded by such offal, to be encased in a dung-heap, to be buried beneath such rot, such loamy, disgusting rot. No, I simply refuse, he said, this is unacceptable, such low-quality soils, simply unacceptable soils. Not even dirt, he said, all gravel and twigs, not even worthy of the name, not worthy for any grave, not sufficient for even an unmarked grave, not even for the lowest of men, not even for a criminal, a fiend. I refuse, he said, no, I simply refuse, nothing of this sort for my grave, absolutely not. It's my grave, he said, I know what kind of soil I want for my grave. Yes, it's my grave, he said, it should have the soil I want for it, and the expense is no matter, the soil is what matters, not the expense, solely the dirt. The soil is what matters, he said, it must be good soil for a good grave, for my grave, good soil for my own grave where I will be buried. No, I insist, I absolutely insist, only the best for my grave, he said, as much as it has to cost, it will cost, and we will pay. I will not settle for just any cheap soil, he said, I will not settle for a cheap local soil, for shit and twigs and bits of rat fur and acorns, for stones and plastic and bits of garbage. Of course, said the woman, we mustn't settle for cheap soil, of course, you're right. She looked at me and smiled in a way I couldn't understand. I didn't want to go to Pittsburgh.

Loss

I'm sorry for your loss. I'm sorry for your loss. I'm sorry for your loss. How many of these do I need to write? *I'm sorry for your loss. Darren was not just a wonderful employee—he was a wonderful man.* A wonderful man. I never met him. Never met this man. *All of us here are so sorry.* Never met any of these guys. *I'm sorry for your loss.* I'm not. I'm not really. *Marianne was an incredible member of the team. We cannot imagine what you and your family must be going through at this time.* Deepest sympathies. Kindest regards. *I'm sorry for your loss. Everyone's loss.* Who were these people? How many of them? *Stephen was an immeasurable asset.* What the fuck am I even saying. Three hundred? We had that many people in the Miami office? *I'm sorry for your loss. Lauren was one of our brightest stars.* I have to write three hundred. By hand. We fit that many in Miami? *This horrific tragedy has affected us all.* I hated the Miami office. *I'm sorry for your loss.* It was a horrible building. *I'm sorry for your loss.* It was a horrible office. *I'm sorry for your loss.* Horrible city. *I'm sorry for your loss.* By hand. I didn't know any of these people. *Your husband was a good man.* I bet he wasn't. I bet he was a louse. A piece of shit. An ass-grabber, an ass-kisser. An ass. Total ass. *An incredible tragedy.* A shit-heel. A bullshitter. A *fucking* piece of *shit*. Complete garbage. *I'm sorry for your loss.* I have to write these by hand. *Your*

136

husband was a true leader. Three hundred sacks of garbage washed out to sea. *I'm sorry for your loss. Our loss.* Three hundred. *Your mother was an incredible employee.* They found parts of the bodies up in South Carolina. Arms. Heads. Arms with no fingers. Arms with two fingers. They interviewed some teenagers in Jacksonville who found a whole body washed up on the beach. They called it *radical.* It was *radical* that they found a corpse on the beach, they said. *You and your family are in our prayers.* By hand. *I'm sorry for your loss.* Jesus Christ.

Bugs

I was a bank teller at a bank and every day I went outside to find new bugs. I found bugs on the ground. I found bugs on the street. I found bugs in the garbage. I found bugs on a dead skunk. I found bugs writhing around the inside of a tree that split in half during a windstorm—in the middle of the night there was this incredible cracking sound, like thunder, but there was no rain or anything—it was just the tree snapping in half. The inside was a network of narrow passages and warped wood. It looked like a dirty sponge. I imagined that it had been filled with bugs for weeks, maybe months, maybe over a year, the bugs slowly burrowing through it, setting up colonies—a colony of ants, a colony of beetles, a colony of wasps, a colony of aphids, a colony of termites—and moving around, boring holes in the bark, scooping out the wood and replacing it with mush and piles of larvae and corpses. Then a windstorm came and it was enough to bend the tree so much that it buckled under the weight of itself, the bugs having colonized only so high that the rotten wood was near the bottom, right at head height, so the top of the tree with all of its branches just got too heavy—the wind pushed it and that was it, it snapped in half. The bugs were still writhing around inside when I found it. I could see all the chambers they had eaten out of the wood. I could see the bugs that had been split in half when the tree buckled. I could see their sticky, mangled bodies smeared onto the tops of the striations. Most of the bugs that were split in half were still twitching. They were still half alive, just like the tree—split in half but still alive. They must have been like that, split in half and twitching, for hours, since the tree snapped. I saw the chamber with the ant queen in it and all the larvae she had produced, and a beetle was also in the chamber. It was picking up the larvae and snapping them in half and eating them. There were ants tugging at its legs and the legs of another beetle that was crawling into the chamber, now that everything was all exposed and open. I thought about how I could just reach in and grab all of them—the queen ant, the larvae, the beetles, the ants tugging at their legs—and scoop it all out in one hand. I thought about the time I was a little kid in my grandparents' backyard in California and they made me clean up all the overripe avocados on the ground. I picked up maybe twenty or thirty and threw them one by one over the fence and into the concrete drainage area. I could hear each one *puck* wetly onto the concrete. I picked up a small, leathery one that was squishier than all the others and when I squeezed it, the skin split and bloomed open and a wad of maybe thirty red wrigglers poured out. I felt them squelch between my fingers and then they gushed out this white, stinking juice into my hand. I threw the mass of brown, dripping gunk and writhing worms toward the fence and it "exploded" in the air. It was like a plume, or a spray. My hand smelled like the worm juice the entire afternoon. My hand smelled like the worm juice the entire night. My hand smelled like the worm juice the entire two-day car trip home. I kept washing my hands, scraping bars of soap with my fingernails and letting the soap stay there, then later soaking my hand in hot, soapy water, but nothing helped, nothing got rid of the smell—every time I scratched my face or picked my nose or rubbed my eyes, I would smell it, the same fetid smell, and that was what I thought of when I saw the beetles and the larvae in the tree. I tried to remember the smell of it, but I couldn't. All I could smell was fresh pine sap—some of the ants were stuck in the sap, wiggling their antennae and mandibles. So I put my hand in and scooped out as much as I could—the ants, the larvae, the beetles, the sap, the splinters. I felt it all as this single, fat, wet mass, and squeezed it, and felt it gush and drip between my fingers. I felt the beetles crawl out onto my knuckles through the mangled everything else. There are bugs everywhere. You can go looking for them and find them and now you will know what will happen when you squeeze.

Healthy, Fit, and Fulfilled

It was the weekend and I rode my bike to the river. Someone had set up a ramp for stunts. Kids were ramping their mountain bikes off the ramp and into the river, leaping from the seat at the last minute to try and grab a large knotted rope that was affixed to a tree branch. My bike was a lightweight road bike designed for long-distances at a moderate cadence— I had paid $680 for it, secondhand, and replaced several of its components over time according to my personal needs and preferences in long-distance biking. I was a member of several internet forums dedicated to bicycle riding and maintenance, engaging often in prolonged discussions regarding the relative quality and efficacy of differently manufactured and designed bicycle parts. Riding and maintaining my road bicycle, and, more recently, some other road bicycles I had been building from spare parts, became my primary hobby—I rode my bicycle for my commute and I would go on extended trips on the weekends. At night, I would calibrate and clean my bicycle in the garage, post on the bicycle forums, and plan new routes to ride. I was feeling healthy, fit, and fulfilled by the hobby's cumulative, cross-domain nature— the act of riding was physically rewarding, while the planning, shopping, trading, and maintenance components of the hobby were mentally fulfilling. I slept well, and awoke eager to engage with the various aspects of the hobby, which was a departure from my previous lifestyle marked by prolonged depressive episodes and suicide ideation. In the years prior, I had become obsessed with the idea of death. Whenever the experience of living my life became overwhelming, I would invoke it as a refrain, as a warding spell—it became central to me, a part of me. I carried the absolution of ending my own life with me at all times, through all traumas and joys, large and small. Death was a component in all my thoughts and feelings, a pallor through which I experienced my life, discoloring everything, drowning out all other hues, and in that way, it created for me immense comfort. I obsessed over my own death and the fact that I could, at any minute, bring about my own end. Every question was answerable with death. Every purpose was closed off by death. Every joy and yet, equally, every pain, was mutable by death. In conversations with colleagues or family, I related all topics to death, to the certain doom that all things faced, constant and inviting. I spent my time in cemeteries, examining the names and dates and projecting lost hopes and ambitions that were cut off by an unexpected illness, or constructing in my mind elaborate manifestations of grief and decay, of continual pain and anguish that culminated in necessary, rushed suicides by gun or noose. I took immense comfort in surrounding myself with death—I found community, freedom, an immense openness among headstones, a sense of belonging, a compassionate, mute understanding by generations of similarly hopeless and suicidal forebearers. In their company, I sought cool relief from the hot sun in a shadowed ditch, the dirt against my cheek, the deep, churning soil against my fragile skin. My despair felt impossibly small pressed up against the largeness of the earth and the fact that somewhere in its depths lay every person that has ever died. Then, two years ago, the pallor lifted, and the bicycle took death's place. It became a symbol for a new era in my life—I no longer yearned for death as an escape and instead found purpose and joy in daily life, and the more I filled that daily life with my bicycles, the more I found purpose and joy. However, my life had since returned to shambles due to unexpected personal and professional catastrophe, and so the era of the bicycle had come to a dispassionate end. I rode my bicycle onto the ramp, which warped the front wheel irreparably, and I tumbled over the edge and onto the embankment. I was unable to grasp the rope.

Jumbo Pretzel Poems

I'm pulling out my phone to write notes for my jumbo pretzel book. I like it when my phone suggests the pretzel emoji every time I type pretzel 🥨. I'm feeling calm looking at the little 🥨. I don't feel anxiety about writing or publishing when I look at the little 🥨. I don't think about anything at all. No, maybe I do and I'm just not paying attention.

Scaffolding

I went golfing. I hit the ball. It landed in the hole (=hole in one). I walked ~227 yards to the green place where the hole was that the ball went in. I looked in the...the golf hole, the hole where the ball goes, where mine went. But I didn't see my ball. It was dark in the ball hole. I lay down on the green stuff around the ball hole, on my stomach, and put my face up to the hole. I thought maybe it was just really deep or something and I could reach in up to my elbow and get it. I remembered that was a thing at some places, ball holes that were like a foot and a half deep for some reason. Someone was telling me about that once, at like, a party in college maybe. I remember he leaned back and arced his hand up and then down in front of him with his eyes wide in a look of concentration, like he was reaching into a deep ball hole for his ball. I was thinking about his eyes when I saw a pair of eyes looking up at me from the golf hole. They seemed like a man's eyes, like a human man—not a racoon or anything—so, like, there was a guy under the green zone, looking up at me through the ball hole, and I could hear him breathing. We were really close to each other. It felt good but I was confused. I thought it was all dirt and rocks underneath the green stuff but I guess I didn't really have any good reason to believe that. I imagined a series of intricate tunnels, like, what's that stuff...with the railings...like outside of buildings under construction, or in space ships, like in TV shows...like, rails and platforms and stuff...made of metal...I don't know, that stuff, lots of it, like a facility under the green stuff, with guys walking around. I thought about him walking on these, like, sci-fi pathway things under the golf course, and thought, like, maybe the ball holes were vents or something. It seemed really complex and I felt tired. He said something but I couldn't really hear. It sounded like, "Front edges" or something, but that didn't make any sense. I said, "What" and he said it again at the same volume. I was confused. I thought, *Runt cages? Brunt ledges?* I said, "What" again, but he just sighed and slid this, like, little shutter or something over the bottom of the ball hole. The hole looked normal then, like, small and normal. I wasn't sure whether to worry about my ball or not, if it was okay to leave it there, with the guy or whatever. I thought it was probably okay because I had other balls with me in my briefcase. I stood up and I realized that the green zone, like, the furry ball hole area, was really wet. My shirt was completely soaked through.

National Weather Service has observed or expects wind speeds to reach at least 18 mph

A gust of wind blows me down. It rolls me across the parking lot. I keep trying to stop and stand up but I can't. At the end of the parking lot is a van. The wind blows the back door open. The wind rolls me into the van. The wind blows the door shut. The wind turns the key in the ignition. The wind rolls down the windows. The wind blows the radio on and depresses the accelerator. The wind drives me somewhere. I close my eyes. I feel sunlight on my face. I listen to the radio. The air is blowing through the open windows and I can smell the ocean. The wind is cradling my head. The wind is whispering something. I strain to listen, then I understand. I smile and shake my head, *No, no.* The wind tugs at my shorts. But I don't stop it. I feel good about it. The wind caresses my penis. This is an insanely bad story. But it's true. It's happening right now.

Acknowledgements

Thank you to Alan Good, Andrew Weatherhead, Brian Alan Ellis, Cavin Bryce Gonzalez, Chelsea Martin, Cory Bennet, Crow Jonah Norlander, Dave Eggers, Elizabeth Ellen, Giacomo Pope, Graham Irvin, Joshua Hebburn, Kevin Sampsell, Lars Iyer, Mark Leidner, Megan Boyle, Mike O'Brien, Mike Andrelczyk, Nathaniel Duggan, Nicolette Polek, Sebastian Castillo, Tao Lin, Troy James Weaver, and Yuka Igarashi, and, most importantly, my family.

Zac Smith is the author of this book and some other books and stuff on the internet. Thank you.